I0727062

MYSTERY SOLVED
WHO DID IT?

DORIS M. JONES

WORKBOOK PRESS LLC
187 E Warm Springs Rd,
Suite B285, Las Vegas, NV 89119, USA

Website:	https://workbookpress.com/
Hotline:	1-888-818-4856
Email:	admin@workbookpress.com

Ordering Information:
Quantity sales. Special discounts are available on quantity purchases by corporations, associations, and others.
For details, contact the publisher at the address above.

Library of Congress Control Number:

ISBN-13:   000-0-000000-00-0 (Paperback Version)
             000-0-000000-00-0 (Digital Version)

PUB. DATE: 03/17/2023

Mystery Solved to:
Who Did It?

DORIS M. JONES

INTRODUCTION

Dianne took Teri to meet her Grandparents for the first time. She is very excited. Dianne called to let her Mom know what time they would arrive. Dianne Johnson was told that one of her babies died the day that she gave birth to her Triplets. Nurse Beverly stole baby Teri and gave her, to her sister and brother-in-law.

Dianne later decided to move to Chillicothe after seeing Sheriff John Ridden, an old acquaintance from high school. Dianne spoke to the Judge on behalf of the Douglas' who raised her stolen daughter, when they went to Court. They were put on probation for five years and given a heavy fine. The FBI later found out that there was another suspect and Joseph Alexander may not be the one who killed his Grandfather, Benjamin Alexander. The story ends with many surprises! **But you must first read, Who Did It? The first book, the beginning of the story! Both books are intriguing.**

CONTENTS

CONTENTS (Cont.)

CHAPTER 1

Teri Meets Her Grandparents

Teri didn't know that she had some grandparents still living. Her parents, parents were deceased. This will be very special for all of them.

The Johnsons' have lived twenty years believing their granddaughter was dead. Now that they are finally going to meet her, they can hardly contain their excitement and joy. Dianne sat down to talk with Teri before they visited her parents.

Dianne said, "Honey, my parents are anxious to meet you. For twenty years, we all thought you were dead, although in my heart, there was great doubt that you were dead."

"Mom, I am so sorry for the pain and trauma my parents put you all through. I am just thankful that we found each other. I felt that something, was missing in my life, but I didn't know what it was," Teri said.

"It's evident that your parents did a great job in raising you. I am grateful for that but, they caused me a lot of pain that I would not wish on anyone," Dianne said.

"I love my sisters! When I met them, it was like that void in my life filled up. I can't wait until we can do things together as Triplets. We are going to have a lot of fun catching up," Teri said.

When Dianne and Teri arrived at her parents' home, Teri stopped before they got to the door.

Dianne asked "What's wrong Teri?"

Teri said, "I keep thinking of the pain my parents caused all of you. I pray that they won't hate my parents."

When they went inside Teri went and hugged both of her grandparents. They were overjoyed to see her. And there were many tears! This was a joyous day for all of them.

Teri said, "I apologize for my parents' causing you all so much heartache and pain. I am so happy to meet both of you."

Mrs. Johnson said, "Honey, it was not your fault. You don't have to apologize. Your parents are adults and they know right from wrong. We all make mistakes some greater than others."

Mr. Johnson said, "Don't worry about it. We have you back and right now, that's all that matters."

Mr. and Mrs. Johnson hugged Teri and they were crying. They were so happy that she was alive and that Dianne had her baby back. It's been twenty long years that they have missed time with their granddaughter. The pain from the loss of a child never goes away completely. Dianne suffered the most because she felt that her child was still alive but had no idea of how to prove it.

Dianne said, "Alright now. We didn't come over here to cry. We came so you all could spend some time with Teri before we go to Chillicothe. I will be going up there for a month and if I like it, I will be moving up there so I can be close to all of my girls."

Mrs. Johnson said, "Now that you have found your daughter, we are going to lose ours."

"No Mom! You and dad will have a new place to visit. You know we are only a couple of hours away. Besides all my babies know how to drive so you will be seeing us regularly," Dianne said.

Teri said, "You will definitely see a lot of me. We have a lot of time to make up and get to know and love on each other. I have been doubled blessed."

They were all laughing and hugging each other. This was a joyous moment in the Johnson's home. They now have all three of their grand-daughters. This is a very special moment that they will remember for years to come. Dianne and Teri spent four hours with her Parents. They thanked God over and over for Teri.

Finally, Dianne said, "The fun must end for now, but we will see you all in a month. After that, we will try to make it every 2-3 weeks visiting you all, and you both will visit us."

"That sounds great but we are going to miss you. We will let the rest of the family know what's happened. When you all come back, we will have a family gathering so Teri can meet the rest of her family," Mrs. Johnson said.

Teri said, "That will be great! I will look forward to coming back. I don't know what's going to happen with my parents but I know I have to forgive them."

"Yes, we all have to forgive them. Holding grudges only hurts the one that holds it. I am going to request to speak with the Judge on behalf of your parents," Dianne said. "I really don't want them to go to prison."

Mr. Johnson said, "That's why I love you so much. You have always been concerned about others more than about yourself. You are very special."

Teri said, "Mom, I love you from the bottom of my heart and I thank you for having compassion for my parents. Most people would want them thrown under the prison."

"Well, we raised a young lady with the love of God in her heart. She has always considered others before herself and we are very proud to be her parents," Mrs. Johnson said.

Dianne said, "Trying to get even just causes more pain and problems. Besides your parents seems like very nice people. I am sure they would not have done this on their own. Everyone deserves a second chance."

"You are right. Even honest people make mistakes. We are human but it is important to be able to forgive a person who does something against you," Mr. Johnson said.

Dianne said, "Mom, Dad, we have to get going so we can rest up tonight, and leave early in the morning. I will call when we get there so you all will know that we made it safely."

They hugged each other as they said their good-byes. Dianne had not been away from her Parents since Walter died. This was going to be a big change for her as she decides to start living again. She realizes that Walter would not have wanted her to live the way she has been living. Her family, Keri and Jeri have been telling her that she needed to start dating again and mingling with other people.

Now that she had seen Sheriff John Ridden again and he is single, she thinks that maybe something special will happen between them. She really enjoyed his visit with her and how he took care of her while he was there. He and Walter were so much alike. Dianne is now anxious to get to Chillicothe to see if she might like living there. Sheriff Ridden told her if she came to visit that he would show her around. When Dianne and Teri left her parents' home, they went back to Dianne's condo. They want to get a good nights' sleep and leave early in the morning. When they were on their way to Dianne's place, Teri called Keri and Jeri. They were very excited to hear from Teri and their mom. Just as Dianne was pulling into the garage, they all said, "I love you and we will talk to you later. They did not tell them that they were coming to Chillicothe in the morning."

Dianne still could not believe that she had her other daughter. As they got out of the car, she was starting at Teri.

Teri asked, "Mom what's wrong?"

Dianne started crying uncontrollably. Teri went and put her arms around her shoulders. Now she was crying. After a while, Dianne stopped crying.

Dianne said, "I am so sorry Teri but it still hurts not having you with me. It even hurts more that Walter did not get to see either one of you. I love you so much. We had great plans for you guys and to do things with you all."

"I am here now, and you won't ever have to worry any more. I could not love you any more than if you had raised me. I am so happy that you found me and I love my sisters dearly. Now I am complete," Teri said. "And I have two families."

Dianne said, "Now all of our lives are complete and now we can be truly happy."

At that moment, Teri thought that she must be the luckiest person in the world. Her biological mother had found her, and she has two Identical Sisters and awesome grandparents. Her blessings are going to be much more than she realizes. Dianne and Teri went into the Condo. They sat down in the living room. Dianne wanted to give Teri some information on how she met her, dad.

"Teri, I want to tell you about your, Dad and how we met," Dianne said.

Teri said, "I would love for you to fill me in about the type of man my, dad was and how you guys met."

We were in college and one night at a football game, there was only one seat available on our side and it was next to Walter. When I was about to sit down, I noticed he was staring at me. So I sat down and looked at him and said, "Hello." And he responded back with, "Hello." "As we were enjoying the game, one of our players' was running for a touchdown. Walter and I just up shouting him on and when we sat down, we looked at each other and started laughing."

"I wish I could have known him," Teri said.

"Any way, Walter asked if I were a student and I told him that I was and he introduced himself. When I told him my name, he thought I was kidding since we were both Johnsons. We laughed. When it was half-time, he asked if I would like to go to the snack bar with him. I accepted. As we walked, he asked if I were dating anyone. I said, "No. I'm not seeing, anyone." We talked throughout the rest of the game. When it was over, he asked if he could walk me to my car. When we got to my car he asked if I would give him my phone number.

"Did you give him your phone number?" Teri asked.

"Yes I did but on the condition, if he called and I requested him not to call anymore, that he would stop calling. He was very nice and polite," Dianne said.

"What was his response to that?" Teri asked.

"Walter told me that if I ever asked him not to call, he would respect my wishes and not call. He let me know that he did not party, use drugs, or alcohol and it turned out we had a lot in common. We were also taking the same classes, just at different times," Dianne said. "He was a very fine and well-mannered young man. He and Sheriff John Ridden are so much alike."

Teri said, "Wow, it would have been wonderful to know him. It sounds like he was a great man."

"That he was and more. He would tell me after we got pregnant that he was going to play with you all. We would laugh about that," Dianne said. "I said, "They will be babies and he said, "They will grow up."

Teri asked, "How did he die? And how long were you all married?"

Dianne said, "It was the same day that you all were born. That morning Walter was trying to get me off my feet. I told him if he didn't get out of here, that I was going to keep him home all day. He finally kissed me and left. Two hours later, two Police Officers were at my door. They told me he had been killed in a car accident. I got hysterical and went into labor. You guys weren't due until two weeks later. One of the Officers got my phone book and called my parents. They realized that I was in labor, so an ambulance was called for me. My parents arrived here at the same time as the ambulance. That was one of the worse days of my life. The second worse day was when Nurse Beverly told me that you died. We were married about fifteen months. They were very happy months too. We loved each other very much."

Teri said, "I think we need to continue this some other time. We both have cried enough lately. Then she asked, "What do you want for dinner? I can cook or make you a sandwich and salad."

Dianne said, "You are right. We have cried enough. A sandwich and salad sounds great since we will be going to bed early. We will need to be on the highway at dawn, so we can beat the heavy traffic."

"Alright, we will have sandwiches and salad," Teri said.

Dianne said, "Thank you, baby."

Teri said, "You are very welcome, mom. I will

do more things with you and for you.”

Dianne said, “If I like Chillicothe, you bet we are going to do a lot of things together and sometimes with your Parents.”

Teri said, “That will be wonderful. I love you, mom. You are the greatest! My parents will be very happy that we all will be able to love each other.”

Dianne asked, “How can I not love the people who took good care of my baby? We are an extended and blended family and you girls will have two sets of Parents.”

Teri said, “Mom, you are an awesome woman and I love you dearly.”

Chapter 2

Joseph Alexander's Arraignment

Sheriff John Ridden was able to get Judge Hewitt from the County of Dallas, Texas to preside over Joseph Alexander's Arraignment. He wanted someone, who had no involvement with the case, to make sure everything was handled lawfully. Since Chillicothe was a small town and most of the citizens knew each other, it was best to get a Judge from the outside.

Judge Hewitt had been on the bench in Dallas for over twenty years. He was known to be as fair, as the evidence would allow him to be and more. He was honest and believed that everyone should be represented, and it should be taken into consideration of the person's background and mental state of mind.

There were times he thought you have to go outside of the box, depending on the situation. Judge Hewitt was well respected by his peers because he was an honest person. Sheriff Ridden called Joseph Alexander's mother Gloria, to let her know his Arraignment date was set for the following week.

Sheriff Ridden asked, "Ms. Alexander will you have a way to get here?"

Gloria Alexander answered and said, "Yes I do. I live about an hour from Chillicothe and I have a car."

Sheriff Ridden said, "We have a few female citizens, who are willing to let you stay at their home as long as you need, to be here for the trial. There are two or three of them that you can pick from, but I think Mrs. Brunswick would be perfect for you."

Gloria Alexander asked, "Sheriff that will be appreciated, because I cannot afford to stay in a hotel. Do you think I could stay at my father's home, since I will want to be here until Joseph's trial is over, or will that be a problem? I would not go into the kitchen or bother anything."

Sheriff Ridden said, "It's still a crime scene, and no one will be allowed in there until this is over. Depending on how the evidence is presented, we may have to go in and reconstruct the crime scene. I am sorry."

Gloria Alexander said, "I understand Sheriff and I really appreciate your call and help."

Sheriff Ridden said, "If you don't have any questions, I will say good-bye for now."

Gloria Alexander said, "I don't have any more questions and thank you again. I will see you Wednesday. I will call and let you know when I am leaving, so you will know about what time I should arrive. Thank you again. Good-bye Sir."

After Sheriff Ridden got off the phone with Gloria Alexander, he called Ms. Stewart.

Ring! Ring! Ring!

Ms. Stewart answered, "Hello Sheriff Ridden. How are you?" She asked.

Sheriff Ridden said, "Ms. Stewart, I am fine, thank you."

"What can I do for you, Sheriff Ridden?" She asked.

Sheriff Ridden said, "I am calling to let you know that Joseph Alexander's Arraignment will be Wednesday starting at 9:00 a.am. After that the Judge will set his trial date."

Ms. Stewart said, "I plan to be there on time."

Sheriff Ridden asked "Since you are a witness, will you please arrive about 8:30 a.m.? You won't have to testify on that day, but you will need to be present. You will testify on the day of his trial."

Ms. Stewart said, "I sure can. I will see you at 8:30 a.m. on Wednesday."

Sheriff Ridden said, "Thank you and I will talk with you then. Good-bye."

Ms. Stewart said, "OK Sheriff. Good-bye."

Deputy Carson went to Joseph Alexander's cell.

He said, "Your Arraignment will be Wednesday. Sheriff Ridden contacted your mom and she will be here. She told Sheriff Ridden that she will let him know when she is on her way."

Joseph Alexander said, "Thank you, Deputy but I wish the Sheriff would not have called my mom. That was her father."

Deputy Carson said, "Sheriff Ridden knows that but you are a young man and he feels that you need your Mom here. Mr. Alexander was her father but you are still her child."

Joseph Alexander said, "I know and wish I could go back. I feel so bad because I not only cause a man's death but he was my grandfather."

Deputy Carson said, "Son you can't go back, but you are going to have to forgive yourself, in order to go forward. Your mom is hurting not only for her father, but for you also."

Joseph Alexander said, "Deputy Carson, I know

and I appreciate you taking time to talk with me. Thank you kindly."

Deputy Carson said, "You are welcome. I must get back to work now, but don't beat your-self up too much. This time will pass and hopefully give you a new outlook on life, so you will do better later in life."

Joseph Alexander said, "Thank you again Deputy Carson. I appreciate your kind words."

Deputy Carson, "I will talk with you later."

Just as Deputy Carson came back from Joseph Alexander's cell, Deputy Ryan came in the office.

Deputy Ryan said, "Good morning Deputy Carson.

Deputy Carson said, "Good morning Ryan."

Deputy Ryan said, "I was in the market this morning and overheard Mrs. Rothchild talking to the Cashier about the Alexander Case."

Deputy Carson asked, "What caught your ear?"

Deputy Ryan said, "Well Mrs. Rothchild said she saw a man come from behind Mrs. Brunswick's home the day of the murder, and she said it was not Joseph Alexander. She said that she saw a different man. He was a little bigger and older than Joseph Alexander."

Deputy Carson asked, "Are you sure you heard her correctly?"

Deputy Ryan said, "I was standing right by her, so I told her that she needs to come in and talk with Sheriff Ridden. She said she was on her way to an appointment, and as soon as it was over, she would be here."

Deputy Carson asked, "Do you think he could have been in Mr. Benjamin's house too?"

Deputy Ryan said, "It's possible. Maybe he was already in the house when Joseph Alexander showed up and couldn't get out, so he hid in the house."

Deputy Carson said, "You just might have something there. Suppose this man was already in Mr. Benjamin's house and he didn't know it? So when Joseph Alexander came in he could not get out. After Joseph left, suppose he killed Mr. Benjamin and when the Triplet came to the door, that was when he left."

Deputy Ryan said, "That sounds feasible. Remember Joseph Alexander said Mr. Benjamin had a lot of money in his wallet. He said he took two hundred dollars and threw the wallet on the table. When we got there, there was no money in his wallet and it was on the floor."

Deputy Carson said, "We need to talk with Sheriff Ridden. We need to go back in that house, and look for finger prints in all the closets and on Mr. Benjamin's wallet."

Deputy Ryan said, "This means that Joseph Alexander may not have killed his Grandfather."

Deputy Carson said, "We will only talk to Sheriff Ridden about this. He should be in the office within the next hour. You know in small towns like this, most people don't lock their doors."

Deputy Ryan said, "You know we could be right. All crimes are not always the way they seem."

Deputy Carson said, "You are so right. A lot of innocent people have been sent to prison, for crimes that they did not commit."

Just as they finished talking, Mrs. Rothchild came through the door and Sheriff Ridden was about two minutes behind her.

Mrs. Rothchild said. "Good afternoon Deputies. I am here to make a statement. I saw a man come from behind Mrs. Brunswick's home, the day Benjamin was killed."

Sheriff Ridden said, "Mrs. Rothchild, we have the man that came from behind Mrs. Brunswick's home."

"Well Sheriff, I heard that you arrested a young man for Benjamin's death. This was not a young man that I saw. He was heavy and an older man.

Boy was he in a hurry," Mrs. Rothchild said.

Deputy Carson asked, "Do you remember about what time it was?"

Mrs. Rothchild said, "I sure do. I had just came out of my door when my alarm went off at 3:00p.m., reminding me to take my medicine. That's when I saw him."

Sheriff Ridden said, "Mrs. Stewart said she saw a young man, come from behind Mrs. Brunswick's home at 2:57 p.m."

Deputy Carson said, "Joseph Alexander is a young man. So, who really killed Mr. Benjamin?" He asked.

They took Mrs. Rothchild's statement, and she left.

Sheriff Ridden said, "I am calling the FBI in with their forensic team, to go over Benjamin Alexander's house, with a fine-tooth comb. If someone else was in his home, then there probably are some other prints. I will ask them to check the pantry as well as all the closets."

Deputy Ryan said, "Deputy Carson and I have a scenario, about what may have happened. If it is correct, that will explain why two different women saw two different men, coming from behind Mrs. Brunswick's home."

Sheriff Ridden said, "I am ready to hear what you guys came up with because right now, everything points to Joseph Alexander."

Deputy Carson asked, "Do you remember that I told you, that Mr. Benjamin's wallet was empty?" Joseph Alexander said he only took $200 from the wallet and when we arrested him, he only had $170 in his pocket. He made a statement that Mr. Benjamin had a wallet full of money, but he only needed a little. He said he took $200 and threw the wallet on the table. When I went in Mr. Benjamin's home, his wallet was on the floor near the pantry, and it was empty."

Deputy Ryan said, "The pantry is probably the

area, the other man was hiding. Mr. Benjamin and a lot of other folks around here, never lock their home up when they go to the market or bank or while they visit a neighbor."

Sheriff Ridden asked, "What are you getting at?"

Deputy Carson said, "I figured that maybe this other man, had come in Mr. Benjamin's house while he was gone. When he heard him come in the house, he may have hid in the pantry. Then Joseph Alexander came over and since they were in the kitchen, the man in the pantry could not leave. But when Joseph Alexander tussled with Mr. Benjamin and took $200 from his wallet, he fell and hit his head on the table. When Joseph bent to check on him, the Triplet was at the door, so he fled out the back through the fence. Then the man in the pantry came out and hit Mr. Benjamin in the head with a blunt object. He took all the money in his wallet, and when he heard the Triple at the door, he threw the wallet on the floor. Then he fled out back through the fence."

Sheriff Ridden said, "You all could possibly have something here. Teri is coming with Dianne. She said she could recognize the man, that went through the fence. After she gets here, I will put Joseph in a line up, with some of the citizens, and see if she recognizes him."

Deputy Carson said, "That's a great idea. We need to check Mr. Benjamin's pantry for a weapon and prints."

Sheriff Ridden said, "I am going to call my friend at the FBI Office and see if he can send some Agents over tomorrow."

Deputy Carson said, "I will have the report that I made ready for the FBI. They can read it, and then go to Mr. Benjamin's home and check things out."

Sheriff Ridden said, "Be ready to answer questions also, because they are very thorough in their investigations. Write out what you and

Ryan think may have happened too. It's not impossible. If there is more evidence, they will find it. Those men are trained to find a needle in a haystack."

Deputy Carson said, "I will type it at home and bring it in the morning. It's time for me to clock out. See you all in the morning."

Deputy Ryan said, "Have a good night."

Sheriff Ridden said," See you in the morning, bright and early."

Finally Joseph Alexander will have his day in Court. He is worried that his mother is going to hate him. Last night, he did not sleep well. He cried most of the night. He knew what he did was wrong, but he never intended to hurt his, grandfather.

Wednesday morning Sheriff Ridden called Gloria Alexander, to make sure everything was alright with her, and that she would be there, when the Arraignment started.

Gloria Alexander said. "Sheriff I will be there in about fifteen minutes, and everything is fine. I appreciate you checking."

Sheriff Ridden said, "It's not a problem. I didn't want Joseph to be by himself. He is so young and that was his, grandfather."

Gloria Alexander said, "This has been very hard for me. I have been praying and asked God to take over. I never thought that I would be facing anything like this."

Sheriff Ridden said. "I understand but we never know what trials we will encounter in life. God is the only one, that we can truly depend on. Mrs. Brunswick is a widow, and she would like for you to stay as long as needed. She is a very nice older woman and I have known her over four years. When you get here, I will introduce you to her, at the Courthouse."

Gloria Alexander said, "I don't know how to thank you all, for your kindness. I have been praying because I didn't know what to do."

Sheriff Ridden said, "We must help each other because one day, we may need help. You will love Mrs. Brunswick and she keeps a very clean house. I will see you later."

Gloria Alexander said, "Thanks again. I will see you soon."

Sheriff Ridden called Mrs. Brunswick to let her know that Gloria Alexander, accepted her invitation to stay at her home. He told her that he would introduce them, at the Courthouse before the Arraignment starts.

After Sheriff Ridden got off the phone with Mrs. Brunswick, Deputy Carson came into his office.

Deputy Carson said, "Deputy Ryan is getting ready to take Joseph Alexander to the Court House. They are about the same size, so Ryan brought some of his clothes for him to wear and shoes."

Sherriff Ridden said, "Thank you. I spoke with his, Mother a little while ago. She will be here, any minute now. Mrs. Brunswick offered to put her up while she is here."

Deputy Carson said, "That was nice of her. My heart goes out to Joseph Alexander, because Mr. Benjamin was his, grandfather and his mothers' father. Something like this would be hard on any family."

Sheriff Ridden asked, "How is he holding up? I am sure that he feels that he is alone in this world."

Deputy Carson said, "Ryan said he had been crying all morning."

Sheriff Ridden said, "He didn't want me to call his mother but I felt that he needed her despite the situation."

Deputy Carson said, "I feel the same way. He seem like he was brought up well. He is very polite and well-mannered."

Sheriff Ridden said, "I could tell that, when I spoke with him. He's not a street kid. Just one of those things where a nice person, made a mistake and it turned out terrible.”

Deputy Carson said, “I am praying that what me and Deputy Ryan came up with, will at least prove that he didn’t kill Mr. Benjamin.”

Sheriff John Ridden said, “That would truly be a Miracle. It happens sometimes.”

“What happen sometimes?” Asked Deputy Ryan.

Deputy Carson said, “Miracles!”

Deputy Ryan asked, “What Miracle are you looking for?”

Deputy Carson said, “I was telling Sheriff Ridden that I have been praying for one for Joseph Alexander.”

Deputy Ryan said, “The more I think about what we came up with, could be a strong possibility of what happened. I couldn’t hardly sleep last night, thinking this might be true.”

Sheriff Ridden said, "I called my FBI friend, Joe Smith. He and some Agents will be here about 10:00 a.m. Ryan, I told him that you would be here, to take him to Benjamin Alexander's home. I will be in and out of the Court House, so I need Deputy Carson to be there to keep me updated. I will introduce Gloria Alexander to Mrs. Brunswick at the Court House."

Deputy Ryan said, "OK Sheriff, I will be happy to take the FBI Agents to Mr. Alexander's home."

Sheriff John Ridden said, "Deputy Carson give Deputy Ryan the paper, that I asked you to write up, of you all's suspicions. I want him to give it to Joe when he gets here. This way, he will know what and where he should be looking for other evidence, if any exists. Make sure he gets the evidence bag with Mr. Benjamin's wallet in it."

Deputy Ryan said, "I will make sure he gets all the evidence that we have Sheriff."

Sheriff Ridden said, "Then I will let Judge Hewitt

know, that I have requested for the FBI to look, into this case. Deputy Carson, I think it will be a good idea for you to give me a copy of you all's statement so I can give it to the Judge. If Joseph didn't kill his, Grandfather, I would hate for him to be sent to prison."

Deputy Carson said, "I am sorry that Ryan and I didn't think of this earlier. I hope the Judge don't have objections to the letter and will be willing to wait for the FBI report."

Sheriff Ridden said, "I don't think we will have a problem with him. I was told that he is the most honest and fair Judge around."

Deputy Carson said, "That's good to know. I had better get Joseph Alexander over to the Court House."

Sheriff Ridden said, "Deputy Carson since I am ready to go to the Courthouse, I will go with you."

Deputy Carson said, "Thanks. I will go now and

get Joseph. His mom may be here already."

When Deputy Carson brought Joseph Alexander in the waiting room of their Police Station, Sheriff Ridden was waiting for them. He could see that Joseph Alexander had been crying a lot. His eyes were almost bloodshot red.

Joseph Alexander said. "Good morning Sheriff. Then he asked, "Did you talk with my mom?"

Sheriff Ridden said, "Yes I did and she will be in the Courtroom on your behalf son, your mother loves you."

Joseph Alexander asked, "How can she love me now, knowing that I killed her, father?"

Sheriff Ridden said, "You are still her baby. Straighten up and keep praying. We have come up with something that might work in your behalf. I can't tell you what it is, but I am having it checked out as we speak."

Joseph Alexander said, "I don't know what it is, but I keep telling myself, that I should have stayed and made sure my, grandfather was not seriously hurt."

Sheriff Ridden said, "Once things happen, you can't go back and change them. You must keep, going forward and pray for the best."

Joseph Alexander said, "Thank you, Sir."

Sheriff Ridden said, "Let's not be late."

When they got to the Court House, Sheriff Ridden went to the Judges' Chamber. He asked Judge Hewitt if he could talk with him a few minutes.

Judge Hewitt said, "Of course come in. Have a seat. What can I do for you this morning?" He asked,

Sheriff Ridden said, "We have a strange case. Joseph Alexander is going on trial for killing his, Grandfather which is his Mother's Dad. He's not a street thug. He's a well-mannered young man who has made a terrible mistake. He didn't want me to contact her. After he found out, his,

Grandfather was dead, he feels that his mother is going to hate him."

Judge Hewitt asked, "What do you need from me? Sometime I can accommodate and sometimes I can't. What do you have here?"

Sheriff Ridden asked, "Will you please let Joseph talk with his mother for about five minutes before the Arraignment start. I think it will be good for both of them. I am begging you, please. We are checking out something that may prove that he did not kill his, grandfather. I brought a copy for you to read after Court today, and you will understand better why I am asking for this. The FBI Agents are checking some things out as we speak. I would appreciate it if you would wait for their report, before making a final decision."

Judge Hewitt said, "You seem like an honest man and you are not trying to bride me. I can do that for you. I don't know if you know my reputation or not, but I am honest and I believe in being fair. I pray before I start Court and I pray after Court is over. I don't ever want to send an innocent man to prison because I want things my way or let someone bride me. I will step down and take off my robe before I do that. Your wish is granted."

Sheriff Ridden said, "Sir, I have heard of your reputation and I respect you on that alone. I am an honest man and would never try bribing a judge or anyone else. Also, I am a praying man and I stand by that. I thank you very much for trusting me."

Judge Hewitt said, "I have an extra room where they can talk in private. Bring them in here."

Sheriff Ridden said, "I truly thank you, Sir. I will bring them in right away."

When Sheriff Ridden went to get Joseph, he first checked to see if his, mom was in the Courtroom. When he went in the Courtroom, a Lady was coming toward him. He figured that had to be Gloria Alexander because she looked like she had been crying a lot. When Gloria saw the Sheriff, she stopped in front of him. Her instincts told her that this was the Sheriff.

Gloria Alexander said, "I am Joseph Alexander's Mother. Then she asked, "Are you Sheriff Ridden? I am so thankful for your help. I love my son."

Sheriff Ridden said, "Yes, I am. I am so happy that you made it. I made arrangements so, you and Joseph can talk in private for five minutes, in the Judges' Chambers."

Gloria Alexander said, "Sheriff Ridden, I thank you sincerely from my heart. I will forever be grateful to you all."

Sheriff Ridden said, "I am going to tell you something, but don't mention it to Joseph. The way Joseph told my Deputies what and how it happened, he may not have killed your, father. I don't want you getting your hope up, but I called in an FBI friend of mine who is at your, Fathers' house now, checking out some new clues. I spoke with the Judge. He is going to wait for the FBI report before making a decision. Hopefully, we will know something later today."

Gloria Alexander almost fainted. Sheriff Ridden caught her before she hit the floor. When she got her composure, he told her to try and stay calm and he will talk to her after Court.

Gloria Alexander said, "You can't imagine how much I have been praying, that my child didn't kill my dad. I know God answers prayers. Thank you, Jesus!"

Sheriff Ridden said, "Yes, He does. You have to keep the Faith and keep praying. Now let me take you to your son. He will be nervous because he thinks you hate him now."

Gloria Alexander said, "He is still my baby and I love him."

Sheriff Ridden said, "That's exactly what I told him. Alright just go in that room over there and Joseph will be brought in. The Judge is allowing you all five minutes. Make them count."

Gloria Alexander said, "Sheriff Ridden, I don't know how to thank you except to keep saying it. Only God knows how much I appreciate you and Mrs. Brunswick."

Sheriff Ridden said, "Go on in and talk with your son. And as soon as my friend gives me his report on his findings, I will let you know his answers. Keep praying and let God handle it."

When Joseph Alexander was brought into the room and saw his mom. He fell to the floor crying. Gloria went to him and held him in her arms crying with him.

Gloria Alexander said, "I love you, Joseph. You are my baby and I will always love you."

Joseph Alexander cried out, "Mom, I am so sorry for what I did. I didn't know he was dead. I didn't try to kill grandpa. When they arrested me and said I was suspicious of killing a man, I didn't know they were talking about grandpa.

I just figured it was mistaken identity. When I told them my name, and they asked if I were related to Benjamin Alexander, I almost died when they said he was dead. So, I thought he must have hit his head, on the table when I snatched his wallet, and he fell. I thought I killed him. That was why I didn't want the Sheriff to call you. I thought you would hate me."

Gloria Alexander said, "I have been praying and asking God to not let it be true. I know my dad is dead and that can't be changed but I don't hate you, Joseph. I love you and I am here for you."

Joseph Alexander said, "I love you, mom and I am sorry that I have hurt you."

Gloria Alexander said, "I have forgiven you and now you have to ask God to forgive you and you will have to forgive yourself."

Just then Deputy Carson came in the room. Deputy Carson said, "I am sorry but it's time to go in for your Arraignment."

Joseph Alexander asked, "What does that mean?"

Deputy Carson said, "That's where charges are read against you, and you will be asked if you are innocent or guilty. The Judge will set a specific amount of money for bail. That means the person will be free until his trial date is set. You don't have to speak at the Arraignment, only answer guilty or not guilty. The Judge will let you know that you have a right to get a lawyer. Later you will be notified of a trial date. If you post bail money and don't show up, the Court will issue a warrant for your arrest, and you lose the bail money. If you don't skip bail, then your mom will get the money back after your trial is over."

Joseph Alexander said, "Mom, I don't want you trying to get money for my bail. I must suffer the consequences for my wrong doing."

Gloria Alexander said, "Let's wait and see what happens. Don't worry about me. Let me worry, about you.”

Joseph Alexander said, “Mom, I don’t deserve anything good now. I have done a terrible wrong, and I am willing to pay the price for it.”

Gloria Alexander asked, “Joseph did I not teach you about God?”

Joseph Alexander answered and said, “Yes you did and I thank you.”

Gloria Alexander said, “Well, trust Him. He is a forgiving God and He knows your heart. I am going in the Courtroom now."

Deputy Carson said, “Come on Joseph, we have to go this way.”

Joseph Alexander said, “Thank you for coming Mom. I love you.”

Gloria Alexander went into the Courtroom and sat down. Sheriff John Ridden was already seated up front. After Deputy Carson brought Joseph Alexander in the Courtroom, and Judge

Hewitt came in shortly afterwards. The Bailiff had Joseph Alexander to stand.

 Judge Hewitt asked, "How do you, plea? Guilty or not guilty?"

Joseph Alexander said, "Guilty Sir. I am sorry and ready to accept the consequences."

Judge Hewitt said, "It's very few people come before me that shows remorse and say they are guilty. I am sure this has caused a lot of grief to your, mother as well to yourself. One important thing to remember before doing a wrong, think who it's going to hurt and what the end might be. Any time a person commits a bad crime, it hurts the whole family."

Joseph Alexander said, "Sir, I appreciate that, and this is something that I will have to live with, for the rest of my life. I never thought that I would find myself in a situation like this. My mom raised me well and my, grandfather was a big influence in my life also. I am praying that God will forgive me."

Judge Hewitt said, "I want you to know that I am a very fair Judge. You will get notification of your trial day. This is where all the evidence that the Sheriff has, will be presented against you. There will be twelve people on the jury and they will decide your faith. Then I will have to take everything into consideration according to the law, to determine what kind of sentence I will give you."

He asked, "Joseph do you understand all of this?"

"Joseph Alexander said, "Yes, I understand Sir. "And thank you kindly Sir."

Joseph Alexander's case was first to be heard. It was only about fifteen minutes long. Deputy Carson took Joseph Alexander back to jail afterwards. In the meantime, Sheriff Ridden was about to introduce Gloria Alexander to Mrs. Brunswick.

Sheriff Ridden went to Gloria Alexander then Mrs. Brunswick went and joined them.

Mrs. Brunswick said, "Hello Sheriff Ridden. And then she asked, "You must be Gloria Alexander? I am looking forwards to sharing my home with you. You don't need to be alone during a time like this."

Gloria Alexander said, "Yes, I am. It's a pleasure, to meet you. I really appreciate the kindness and hospitality you have extended to me."

Mrs. Brunswick said, "It's no problem. It will be nice to have someone in the house with me."

Sheriff Ridden said, "I will let you ladies go on and get acquainted. I want to meet with a friend who is checking something out for me. Ms. Alexander, I will talk with you later."

Gloria Alexander said, "Thank you again Sheriff. You have given me some hope. May God bless you."

"Judge Hewitt will let Joseph Alexander stay in jail until the FBI completes their investigation." Sheriff Ridden said, "If you can stay a few days, I will let you visit with Joseph."

Gloria Alexander said, "I would love that, if Mrs. Brunswick doesn't mine."

Mrs. Brunswick said, "Of course, I don't mind. You can stay as long, as you want too. If you must leave, just let me know the day you will be back, for Joseph's trial. You will always be welcome at my home. If he gets a quick trial date, you can stay until it's over."

Gloria Alexander hugged Mrs. Brunswick and said, "May God forever bless you."

Sheriff Ridden said, "Ms. Alexander, I will call you either later this evening or tomorrow morning. I will have more information on what I told you earlier. You ladies have a wonderful evening."

"Sheriff and Mrs. Brunswick, please call me Gloria."

They said bye to Sheriff Ridden at the same time. As he was leaving, he looked back and waved at them. He was thinking, "I would hate to have gone through something like this," Your own child killing one of your parents. That can cause deep emotional pain."

Mrs. Brunswick told Gloria to follow her to her home. She has a two car garage where Gloria can park her car. When they got in front of Mrs. Brunswick's home, she motioned for Gloria to go in first, after she opened the garage with the remote control. When they got in the house Mrs. Brunswick showed Gloria her spare bedroom.

Gloria Alexander said, "You have a beautiful home and this room is gorgeous. It looks like a room from a magazine. I love it!"

Mrs. Brunswick said, "Make yourself at home. I want you to know that I am not a nosey old lady. If you want to or need to talk about anything, I am here for you. I don't ask personal questions unless it's something that you are sharing with me. I want you to be relaxed here and don't be waiting for me to start drilling you about your business. That's not what I do. I just wanted to be up front with you. If you want to lie down it's fine. If you are hungry, the kitchen is yours. You don't have to ask for anything."

Gloria Alexander said, "Mrs. Brunswick, you can't know what your kindness means to me. Only God knows how thankful I am. I had no idea of how or where I was going to live while I am here. Sleeping in my car was the only option I had, but I prayed and trusted God. He answered my prayers way beyond my expectation."

Mrs. Brunswick said, "Don't ever underestimate what God can and will do for you. He will surprise you every time. I will let you get some rest. I will start dinner about 4:00 p.m."

Gloria Alexander said, "I will be happy to help you cook."

Mrs. Brunswick said, "Thank you, but it will be simple and quick. Once it's done, you will be able to eat when you are ready. But if you are hungry now, I can fix sandwiches and salad."

Gloria Alexander said, "Only if you let me fix the sandwiches and you make the salad."

Mrs. Brunswick said, "Now you are talking. Let's get going."

They both laughed and Gloria hugged Mrs. Brunswick and thanked her again for her kindness. They fixed their lunch and laughed and talked.

Gloria Alexander was very thankful for the kindness that was shown to her. She was glad that her, Mom was not alive to see her grandson being charged for killing her husband. Gloria is thinking after this is over, she will move here. She has been looking for a nice quiet place and this is perfect because the residents are nice too. She and Joseph can live in her, Dad's home. It was paid off.

CHAPTER 3

The Triplets Together

Dianne and Teri got up early so they could get on the road to Chillicothe. Dianne decided to call Sheriff John Ridden on his cell phone, since they were leaving before, he would be in the office.

At Sheriff Riddens' home, his cell phone rang. Ring! Ring! Ring!

He answered and said, "Hello."

Dianne said, "Hello John. Sorry for waking you."

Sheriff John Ridden asked, "Is everything alright?" Are the Triplets ok? "

Dianne said, "Everything is fine. I am calling to let you, know that Teri and I are on our way to Chillicothe. I didn't call my girls. We are going to surprise them. This will be the first time the girls will be together, beside the little time, they had at the Court House. I am so excited for them. It's going to be something having them together."

Sheriff John Ridden said, "I am glad you guys are alright. Then he asked, "About what time do you think you all will arrive?"

Dianne said, "We should be there in about an hour. We got a head start on the traffic."

Sheriff John Ridden said, "Be safe and call me when you get here."

Dianne said, "OK John. I will see you later. Bye for now."

Sheriff Ridden said, "See you later."

He is wired up now that Dianne is coming to Chillicothe like she promised. He told her that he would show her around the area.

Dianne is thinking, "I am beginning to feel like a school girl. I am excited that am going to be able to spend time with John. I can't Believe that we have crossed paths again. I never thought that John Ridden and I would see each other again."

Teri asked, "Mom do you want me to drive now?"

Dianne said, "Honey I am fine if I feel tired I will let you take over."

Teri said, "I can hardly wait to see my sisters."

Dianne said, "I know all three of you are going to be happy together. I just keep thanking God for letting me find you. I love you so much."

Teri said, "Mom, I have been thanking God for letting me find my family. For years, I had no idea of what was missing in my life. It's been like a puzzle. Since we got together and I saw my sisters, it's like a missing piece of a puzzle was put in place."

Dianne said, "I am also thankful that you had good people taking care of you."

Teri said, "I am just sorry that we have missed

so much time being apart. All these years, I have felt an emptiness in my life. I was always wondering why I felt like that."

Dianne said, "I believe God is going to give us a lot of time together. The girls are going to be ecstatic when they see us. I promised them that I would go to Chillicothe and stay a month and if I liked it, I would move there."

Teri said, "Mom that will be great if you move there. Then we all can spend a lot of time together. I am going to be so happy having two families. Once you get to know my parents I know you will love them."

Dianne said, "I love them already. I can tell that they are decent and loving people by the way they loved and cared for you."

Finally they have reached the city of Chillicothe. Dianne picked up her phone to call Sheriff Ridden.

Ring! Sheriff Ridden asked, "Are you all here?"

Dianne said, "Yes, and we are headed to my girls. They are really going to be surprised. Since my girls are here, I have decided to move here."

Sheriff Ridden's heart started pounding in his chest. It was so loud that he thought Dianne might hear it. His mind was racing over everything they talked about when he was in Dallas at her place.

Sheriff John Ridden asked, "Are you serious?"

Dianne Johnson said, "I have never been more serious in my life. And my best friend is here also. The girls are calling in. I will talk with you later. Bye for now."

Sheriff John Ridden said, "You will love it here once you get settled. I will talk with later. Bye."

Dianne and Teri went on to Keri and Jeri's apartment. People will have to stop referring to them as Twins. It was a Saturday morning and Keri and Jeri had been up for about thirty minutes. The doorbell rang and they looked at each other in wonderment. They wondered who was ringing their doorbell this early in the morning. Keri said, "I will get it."

When she opened the door, she was surprised. She started screaming. Jeri came running in the living room and she saw why Keri was screaming and crying. Jeri started screaming and crying. They could not believe that their Mother had finally come to Chillicothe. By now Teri and Dianne were crying and laughing. They all ended up laughing and hugging each other.

Keri said, "Why didn't you call us and let us know that you all were coming?"

Teri said, "Then it would not have been a surprise."

Keri said, "I don't believe Mom is really here. Wow! We have been trying to get her here for ages."

Jeri said, "She is finally here and our sister. This is the best surprise one could ever wish for."

Dianne said, "Alright ladies, we need to get our things out of the car and get settled in."

Teri said, "Mom take a seat and we will get the things out of the car."

Keri said, "Teri, you take a seat too. Jeri and I will get your bags out of the car."

Jeri asked, "What do you all want for breakfast? Or do you all want to go out to eat?"

Teri asked, "Do you have food in the kitchen?"

Keri said, "We have plenty of food."

 Dianne said, "Well that solves it. We will cook some of your food."

Jeri said, "You guys sit down. You just got off the road traveling. We will fix breakfast for all of us."

Dianne said, "We will appreciate it. Whatever you fix will be fine with me."

Teri said, "You all should know that I like whatever you all like."

They all laughed. Dianne had not stopped thanking God for letting her baby be alive. Jeri and Keri are so happy that they have their sister. Now they will be able to do things together and go places and confuse people. They are looking forwards to doing that as Triplets.

Teri will see if she can get her job back. She liked working in the pharmacy and the customers loved her too. Keri and Jeri work in Chillicothe. Where Teri worked in Altus is closer to Chillicothe, so her ride will only be 15 minutes instead of thirty minutes. After they finished their breakfast, they prayed together.

Dianne said, "Now that I am here, we have to put together a schedule. I need to know all of your work schedules and you guys can let me know what days that you want to spend with me. In the meantime, I will find out when John will want to show me around. I don't want to be in you all's way all the time. Let me know when we can do family stuff, like the movies, etc."

Keri and Jeri said, "Mom we are so happy that you decided to visit. You will never be in our way."

Teri said, "In a while we all will be talking in threesome. Once we are used to each other and do things together, we are going to drive people crazy."

Keri and Jeri said, "We sure will and we are going shopping so all our clothes are alike."

Teri said, "I bet I already have some clothes like you guys."

All three of them said, "I am so happy that we are together. I love you guys."

Dianne asked, "Ok guys what are we going to do today?"

"We can just kick it around the house," the Triplets said.

Of course, they all laughed.

Dianne said, "Oh boy! I will be the one who goes crazy first. I am going to have to get used to this, but it's going to be fun. I have all three of my daughters. I love you all so much."

"We love you too mom, and we are going to have fun together," the Triplets said.

Dianne said, "Excuse me girls, I promised to call John when we got here."

Dianne went in the bedroom and closed the door. She dialed Sheriff Ridden phone while feeling a little anxious.

Ring! Ring! When he answered, he heard the sweetest voice.

Dianne said, "Hello John. Teri and I have settled in with the girls."

Sheriff Ridden said, "Dianne, I am glad you all made it safely. Have you made any plans for this evening?"

Dianne said, "No, I don't have any plans."

Sheriff Ridden asked, "Can you get away for a couple of hours later? I would like to see you."

Dianne said, "That won't be a problem. And then she asked, "Is 7:00 p.m. a good time for you or do you want to come earlier?"

Sheriff Ridden said, "I can be there about 6:00 p.m. if that's a good time for you."

Dianne said, "I will see you then, bye."

Sheriff Ridden said, "Later."

When Dianne got off the phone with Sheriff John Ridden, she went in the living room where her daughters were sitting and talking.

Dianne said, "I hope you all won't mind, but Sheriff Ridden is coming to get me this evening."

Keri and Jeri said, "Good. You won't be stuck in the house now."

Dianne said, "I plan to spread my wings a little. I am not going to be in you all's way. I don't want you guys to feel like, you have to entertain me. I am a big girl!"

Teri asked, "And what time are you expecting him?"

Dianne said, "About 6:00 p.m. I will only be gone a couple of hours."

The Triplets said, "You don't have to rush."

There is going to be a lot of laughter in this household, because every time they speak in unison, they laugh. Dianne's heart is racing now. She is going to spend the evening with Sheriff Ridden. The excitement is about to get the best of her. Now she had to decide what she was going to wear.

She finally settled for a black pair of straight leg jeans, which showed her curves real good. She wore a white T-shirt and a pair of white tennis. She looked like a teenager. The weather was nice for an evening out. When she went in the living room where the Triplets were, they turned around in awe!

"Mom, you look like a teeny bopper," the Triplets said at the same time.

Dianne started laughing.

She said, "Do I look alright? Do I need to change to something more conservative?"

"Oh no! You look perfect. Sheriff Ridden is going to be all over you," the Triplets said.

They all started laughing almost uncontrollable.

CHAPTER 4

Dianne Loves Chillicothe

Sheriff Ridden arrived at the Triplets apartment at 6:00 p.pm. When the doorbell rang, Dianne started toward the door. The Triplets jumped up at the same time.

They said, "Oh no! You go in the bedroom. We will answer the door."

Dianne could not help but laugh. The girls were so serious.

Jeri said, "Mom when you are going on a date, you don't answer the door, if someone else is in the house with you."

Dianne said, "Girls, it's not a date. He is an old friend."

Keri said, "We are going to have to work out a system, for us to talk when we are together, so we don't talk at the same time. Right, now I am going to answer the door."

Keri opened the door and said, "Hello Sheriff Ridden. How are you doing?"

Sheriff Ridden said, "I am doing great thank you. I am here to see Dianne."

Keri said, "Come in Sheriff and have a seat. I will let Mom know that you are here."

Jeri and Teri said, "Hi sheriff Ridden."

Sheriff Ridden said, "Hello ladies."

Teri and Keri went into the room to get Dianne. She looked so beautiful and with her hair down.

Sheriff Ridden stood up when she entered the living room. His eyes lit up when he saw her. She was a knock out! All he could think about, if he would have said something to her, while they were in high school. They would have married and would still be married. He loved her from the first day that he saw her.

Dianne said, "Hi John. I am ready to go."

Sheriff Ridden said, "You are beautiful."

Dianne said, "Thank you, John. Girls I will be gone for a couple of hours. See you all later."

The Triplets stated jumping up and down laughing after Dianne and Sheriff Ridden left.

Jeri and Keri said, "Watch out! This is Mom's first date since Dad died. Sheriff Ridden is a very special man."

Teri said, "It would great if he becomes our dad."

Keri and Jeri said, "Dad! That sounds great. We have never had our dad."

They both hugged each other while crying. Teri walked over and hugged them and she started crying. They didn't get to know their dad. He was killed in a car accident a few hours before they were born. Dianne never dated after his death. The Triplets stopped crying and hugged each other. They all were wondering what kind of system they use, so they don't always talk at at the same time. Keri broke the silence.

She said, "It's three of us, so we will be numbers, in the order that we were born. I am #1, Jeri is #2 and Teri is #3. When we are together, we will look at each other and hold up the finger or fingers of who should speak."

Jeri said, "If someone asks a question, we will hold up the finger, who we feel can best answer it. If it pertains to one of us particular, then that finger # will be held up."

Teri said, "Or if one has spoken, then one of the other two can take turns talking. That way, one person is not always talking."

Keri said, "We are going to have to work on it, to see if it will work. When mom comes home tonight, we will try it on her."

Jeri said, "This is going to be the beginning of Triplet fun."

They started laughing. Dianne got home that night about 9:30 p.m. Sheriff Ridden stayed on the porch. He kissed Dianne on the cheek.

Dianne asked, "What was that for?"

Sheriff Ridden said, "For making my evening pleasant. I enjoyed our conversation and time together."

Dianne said, "John, I thank you. It was kind of like old times. I always enjoyed being in your company."

Sheriff Ridden asked, "Is it ok to call you tomorrow?"

Dianne said, "John, you don't need permission to call me. You can call me any time, day or night."

Sheriff Ridden said, "You are wonderful! Thank you and now I am going to say good night."

Dianne said, "You are great yourself. Good night, John. I will talk with you tomorrow."

The Triplets were up and waiting for their, Mom to come inside. When Dianne walked inside, they were lined up in front of the door. Dianne started laughing when she saw them.

Dianne asked, "Are you guys waiting to grill me?"

They looked at each other and Keri held up one finger.

Keri said, "Yes mom. "Was your evening nice with Sheriff Ridden?" She asked.

They looked at each other and Jeri held up two fingers.

Jeri asked, "Where did you all go."

Dianne said, "We went to his home. He wanted me to see where he lived. We watched TV and talked about our past, Denise who was my best friend, and we talked about our other friends."

They all looked at each other and Teri held up three fingers.

 Teri asked, "Do you think you all will have more dates?"

Dianne said, "That wasn't a date. We are old friends catching up on missed years. And she asked, "What is it with these fingers?"

They looked at each other and Keri held up one finger.

Keri said, "We are trying to work out a system so we don't always talk at the same time. Our numbers are in the order that we were born."

She explained their system that they were trying out.

Dianne said, "That is interesting but keep trying it on me before doing it with anyone else. I want to see how effective it is."

They all laughed and the Triplets said, "We think we can work it out."

Dianne said, "John drove around town and on the outskirts of town so I could see the different areas. I believe I will go home in two weeks and start packing. I will keep the Condo so when we visit Dallas, we will have our own space."

The Triplets started shouting and laughing and hugging Dianne.

They said, "And we will be a family."

Dianne said, "There is no way that I would be able to stay away from you guys now that we have Teri. We have a lot of years to make up."

Teri held up three fingers.

Teri asked, "Mom, if you go on a weekend, we can go and help you pack, the things that you want to bring here?"

Dianne said, "I need to look for a place while I am here. I want at least three bedrooms, so when my Parents visit you guys can stay at the house with us if you want too."

Jeri held up two fingers and said, "That sounds wonderful mom."

Keri held up one finger and asked, "Mom, what about your job?"

Dianne said, "I will be able to work from home.

When I was in Dallas, I didn't want to work from home. I lived alone and I would not have gone out and mingled with other people. Here I will be able to see you guy regularly and John and I will make new friends."

Dianne and Sheriff Ridden started spending a lot of time together. Sometimes in between her work, she would go to the Police Station, and answer the phones when they were busy.

The girls were getting used to Sheriff Ridden being at their place. Dianne had him over for dinner some evenings. They all were getting to know each other on a personal basis. He even came over some Saturday evenings and watched movies with them. Dianne thought this would have been the way, Walter would have spent time with the girls, had he lived. The girls weren't really dating. They had girl friends that they spent time with. Sometimes, they went to the movies, bowling, and sometimes to a club. They had some male friends, but they were co-workers and neighbors, none serious.

Dianne wondered which one would fall in love first and marry. By them being Identical, she wondered if they did get married would it create a problem for them. One evening she sat the Triplets down to talk to them about dating.

Dianne asked, "I know you all are still young, but have you been thinking about what's going to happen, when you guys start dating?"

All three of them raised their fingers and they laughed.

Dianne said, "We will start with Keri and go in order."

Keri said, "I wonder about it a lot, but I haven't met a guy that I want to date."

Jeri said, "I have thought about it at different times, but if I date, the guy he has to like my sisters and my, Mother."

Teri said, "I dated two guys for a very short while. I didn't like either one of them for a serious relationship. I think it's something that we need to pray about, so God will put the right man in each of our lives."

Dianne said, "Well there is an Organization for Multi Births. Maybe you all should look it up and see what happens. Maybe you all will meet some Identical male Triplets. They would understand the closeness you guys have with each other, and you all would understand the closeness that they have with each other. Think about it."

The Triplets said, "OK mom. It sounds interesting. We will check into it."

CHAPTER 5

The Douglas' Probation

The Douglas' called Teri again to let her know what day they would go before the Judge. It was Monday morning. Teri was getting ready for work when she heard her phone. Ring! Ring! Teri answered and said, "Hello!

Mrs. Douglas asked, "How are you, baby?"

Teri said, "Mom it's so good to hear your voice. I am fine. I miss you and dad"

Mr. Douglas said, "Teri its' dad."

Teri started crying. She said, "I miss you all so much. I love you, mom and dad."

Mrs. Douglas said, "We love you too and we miss you."

Mr. Douglas said, "We called to let you know that we will go before the Judge on Wednesday. Please let Ms. Johnson know because she wants to speak with the judge on our behalf."

Teri said, "I will let her know and I will come with her. I want to see you all."

Mrs. Douglas said, "We want to see you too. This has been very hard on us. We are thankful that you have your mom and sisters so we don't have to worry about you."

Teri said, "They are great and I love them too."

Mrs. Douglas said, "We have to hang up now. We love you. Bye."

Teri said, "I love both of you. Bye."

Dianne came in the room just as Teri got off the phone with her parents.

Dianne asked, "Is everything alright Teri? Was that your Parents on the phone?"

Teri looked at Dianne with tears running down her face. She just shook her head for yes. Dianne walked over to her and hugged her so she would know everything would be alright.

Dianne said, "Everything is going to be fine."

Teri said, "They will go before the Judge on Wednesday. Mom said you wanted to know."

Dianne said, "Yes, I plan to go to their hearing."

Teri said, "Mom, I want to go with you please."

Dianne said, "I was going to ask if you wanted to go. That's not a problem. In fact, it will be good for the Judge to see you there. And it will be good for your parents too."

Teri said, "Mom I love you so much. You are the best."

Dianne later called Sheriff Ridden. She wanted to let him know that she would be out of town a couple of days.

Ring! Ring! Sheriff Ridden answered, "Hello."

Dianne said, "Hi John. I am calling to let you know, Tuesday morning Teri and I will be going to Dallas, for her parents hearing on Wednesday. I am not sure if Keri and Jeri are going but most likely they will want to go also."

Sheriff Ridden said, "I will check my schedule. I will probably be able to go with you all. I will call you later and let you know. There is a call on hold for me. Later."

Dianne said, "That would be great. Later."

Keri and Jeri came in the room just as Dianne hung up with Sheriff Ridden.

Dianne said, "Teri's parents are going for their hearing on Wednesday. Teri and I are going to Dallas to support them. We will leave on Tuesday morning. Sheriff Ridden may be able to drive us there."

Keri and Jeri said, "We want to go too."

Dianne asked, "What about work?"

Keri and Jeri said, "It won't be a problem. Everything is under control at work. Next month is when we will have to grind."

Dianne said, "You all forgot your number thing."

They all started laughing.

Dianne said, "I guess we will all be off to Dallas for a few days. And we can see my Parents and some of the other relatives. I will ask Mom to have them to come to their home, so we don't have to drive around."

Teri said, "I am excited to see some of my other relatives."

Dianne said, "They all are anxious to meet you too."

Just then Dianne's phone rang. Ring! Ring!

Dianne answered, "Hello."

Sheriff Ridden said, "I will be able to drive you all to Dallas and since I haven't had a vacation, I can be off for a few days."

Dianne said, "That's good because Keri and Jeri are going also. We are going to have a family gathering at my parents, so Teri can meet some more of her family. They all want to see her."

Sheriff Ridden said, "That sounds great."

Dianne said, "I was thinking that I could rent a nine passenger van so there will be plenty of leg room."

Sheriff Ridden said, "You don't have to do that. I have a Winnebago Mobile Home. We can drive it. I very seldom use it. I bought it two years ago. I thought I might do some traveling, visiting relatives, but I got busy in the office and never did. I have used it, to go fishing a couple of times on the weekend."

Dianne said, "That sounds like a great idea. On the way back we can stop somewhere and spend the night."

The Triplets said, "Yes, we can make it a mini vacation."

Dianne said, "I think those numbers are going to work very well."

Sheriff Ridden asked, "What numbers?" Is that something new?"

Dianne said, "The girls are trying out a number system, so they don't talk at the same time. Keri is #1, Jeri is #2 and Teri is #3. They will take turns holding up their finger with their number, so they don't speak at the same time."

Sheriff Ridden said. "That is interesting. I will see you guys Tuesday morning. I have a call on hold. Bye for now."

Dianne said, "I will talk with you later. Bye."

This was on a Monday. Dianne was excited knowing that she was going to spend some time with Sheriff John Ridden. Since the girls would be with them, it would be like family.

After she got off the phone with Sheriff Ridden, she turned to the girls and said, "I want you all to wash any dirty clothes that you have, clean your room good, and each of you pack a bag. I want to be ready when it's time to go and no dragging around. When you all pack, make sure you have all your personal hygiene stuff with you."

All three of them said, "Yes ma'am. We will be ready to go in the morning."

Dianne said, "I am going to straighten up in my room. I don't like to come home from a trip and things are out of order. When you all get up in the morning, please make your beds."

Jeri and Keri said, "Mom, you raised us well. We always do those things before we go on a trip."

Dianne said, "It's good to know that."

Teri said, "I have been trained to do that also."

Dianne said, "Three beautiful daughters with good house-keeping skills."

Tuesday morning came quick. The phone was ringing and Jeri said, "I've got it."

Sheriff Ridden said, "Good morning,"

Jeri said, "Good morning, Sheriff Ridden."

Sheriff Ridden said, "Let your, mother know that I am on my way."

Jeri said. "I will let her know. We all are ready."

 Sheriff Ridden said, "Thank you. I will be there shortly. Bye."

Jeri said, "Bye."

Dianne and Keri came into the room. Then Teri followed them. Everyone was up and ready to go. They were so excited about being together as a family now. The Triplets were still overwhelmed, that they are whole now. Dianne hated that Walter wasn't able to see his daughters. He used to tell her how he was going to play with them.

Sheriff Ridden arrived in his mobile home. After he parked, he got out and rang the doorbell.

Dianne said, "Girls, get your bags and make sure your back door is locked and all the windows are closed." She opened the front door and said, "Good morning John."

Sheriff Ridden said, "Good morning beautiful. Let me take your bags."

Dianne said, "Thank you, John. The girls are doing a last minute check of the apartment."

Sheriff Ridden opened a storage compartment on the outside of his mobile home to put their bags in. The Triples came out shortly afterwards.

The Triples said, "This is nice, Sheriff Ridden."

Dianne said, "It is awesome."

Sheriff Ridden said, "I am glad you all like it. It rides good too. Before we get on the road, you all can take a quick tour, and then decide where you want to sit or lay."

After they took their little tour, they got on the road. Teri was getting anxious to see her Parents again. This was the longest that she had ever been away from them. They are the only Parents that she has ever known so it's been hard on her and her Parents. She has not cried since they had been apart.

Dianne sat up front with Sheriff Ridden and the

Triples were in the middle of the mobile home laughing and talking. The girls had some music playing in the background and they played cards.

Dianne said, "John, we really appreciate you helping us through this situation. I really don't know what I would have done without your help."

Sheriff Ridden said, "I thank God that I was able to find you and to be able to help you and the girls. The pleasure is mine."

Dianne asked, "Do you think the Judge is going to give the Douglas' a harsh sentence?"

Sheriff Ridden said, "It depends on the evidence and the Judge. If the Judge is pretty compassionate, there may be some leniency since they didn't orchestra the crime and because they were so desperate for a baby that they couldn't say no."

Dianne said, "I just don't want them to go to

prison. I have tried to put myself in their shoes. Now they are in jail and worried about their child and may lose their life savings for a good lawyer. Teri loves them so much. They raised her real well."

Sheriff Ridden said, "Try not to think too hard about it. Pray and let God handle it. He knows what's best for all of you."

Dianne said, "You are right. I need to just relax and enjoy this ride."

Sheriff Ridden said, "That's more like it. After you get back home, are you planning to look for work, or do you have a plan for your spare time?" He asked.

Dianne said, "Well I had been trying to decide if I want to continue working. Since I can work from home with my job in Dallas and the pay is extremely good and I have good benefits, I think I will keep it."

John Ridden said, "That's a smart move, but

when you need a break or change, you can help in the office, part-time with the phones and some paperwork."

Dianne said, "Wow! I will think about it. It should be nice working for you, Sheriff Ridden."

They started laughing. Sheriff Ridden was thinking, "I am not going to lose you again."

Dianne was thinking, "That will be perfect and there will be no competition. Sometimes we may be able to eat together in the office when things get hectic. He still had the same mannerism as when we were in school."

Finally they reached the Dallas Courthouse. They were able to park in the underground parking. By the time, they got parked and into the Courthouse, they had fifteen minutes before the Douglas' hearing. They all sat up front and Sheriff Ridden let the Bailiff know that Dianne wanted to speak to the Judge on behalf of the Douglas'. Finally, the Douglas' were brought in the Courtroom. They were watching, for Teri and when they spotted her, their eyes lit up with smiles. Teri returned their smiles but she was not allowed to speak to them. In the meantime, the Bailiff came and got Dianne and Sheriff Ridden, so she could speak with the Judge before he decided on the Douglas' case. They were taken into the Judges' Chamber.

Dianne spoke with the Judge.

Dianne said, "Your Honor, I am the mother of the baby that was stolen twenty years ago. I came today to speak on behalf of the Douglas. They were forgiven years ago even though I didn't know who they were. I am here today to ask if you would please have mercy on them. My daughter Teri is with us now. The Douglas' did a beautiful job raising her. I have my Triplets. Teri has two families now who love her very much. I don't believe that the Douglas' were aware of Nurse Beverly's plan to steal a baby. If they are sent to prison for a long period of time, it's going to hurt both families. I have suffered more than enough for the past twenty,

Years feeling that my daughter was alive, but I didn't know what to do. If you send the Douglas' to prison for a long period of time, it's going to cause more pain and heartache to this family. We are tired of crying. That's all I have to say, and I thank you for listening to me."

After Dianne spoke with the Judge, she and Sheriff Ridden went back into the Courtroom. Then Judge Davidson came into the Court and everyone had to stand. Then the Bailiff told everyone to sit down. The Douglas' were instructed to stand before the Judge so he could let them know what he was going to do. When they stood up, everyone was quite.

Judge Davidson said, "This is a very unusual situation. You all had someone else's child for twenty years causing that mother, who is here in the Court today, a lot of pain. By the grace of God, Mrs. Dianne Johnson has spoken with me in my Chambers on your behalf. I must say, if it were my child, I don't know if I could have mercy on you all but she has asked that I have mercy on both of you. I have already read the statements made by the Douglas' and Nurse Beverly. It appears that this devious thing was totally done by Nurse Beverly. Since you all wanted a baby so bad, you did not have the heart to turn away from Mrs. Johnson's baby.

Mr. and Mrs. Douglas, you both know right from wrong, and you knew that Nurse Beverly was wrong when she brought you this baby, but you kept her any way. After reading your statements of remorse and hearing Mrs. Dianne Johnson, the biological mother pleading for you all, I am going to do something that probably has never been done in a case like this. I believe that you all are sincerely sorry, but you still must have, some type of restitution. I am ordering you all to pay Mrs. Dianne Johnson $100,000. Money will never make up for the agony and pain that you caused this mother but I want to hurt your pockets. Also, I want you to take out an insurance policy for one million dollars on Mr. Douglas and make Keri and Jeri, the benefactors, if he dies before them. They are Identical and there was a void in both of their lives not having their sister. They suffered too. Finally, I am releasing both of you today on OR (Own Recognizance) and your probation will be for the next five years. Mrs. Douglas fainted and Mr. Douglas was crying as he caught her before she fell. Judge Davidson said I hope this will deter you from ever doing something that you know is legally wrong again."

Judge Davidson asked, "Mr. Douglas do you have anything to say to Mrs. Dianne Johnson?"

Mr. Douglas said, "Yes, Your Honor. Mrs. Johnson, I sincerely apologize on behalf of myself and my wife. We have done a terrible wrong. We thank you for your forgiveness and also for pleading mercy for us with Judge Davidson. And Keri, Jeri and Teri, we owe you all an apology also. You should never have been separated. I pray that all of you will be able to forgive us. We will go forward and do what we have been instructed to do and pray that God, will forgive us for this terrible wrong."

Judge Davidson said, "Bailiff, release Mr. and Mrs. Douglas so they can go home."

Teri started crying and that set off Keri and Jeri too. They were hugging each other and crying. Sheriff Ridden came and hugged the girls.

 Dianne came up in front of Judge Davidson and said, "Thank you, Judge Davidson. I believe in my heart that you made a righteous call. Thank you."

Judge Davidson nodded as he got up to leave the Courtroom. Dianne walked over to Sheriff Ridden and the girls. Mr. and Mrs. Douglas came over to them and hugged Dianne and thanked her again. Then they hugged Teri for a long time. This was the first time the Douglas' saw all three of the girls together. They started laughing.

Mrs. Douglas hugged Keri and Jeri, then asked, "How am I going to tell you all apart? You all are so beautiful together. I love all of you."

They said, "We know who we are." Everyone laughed.

Dianne asked, "Do you all need to go to Nurse Beverly' home for anything?"

Sheriff Ridden said, "I drove my mobile home and if you guys plan to go back to Altus in the next two days, you are more than welcome to ride back with us."

Mr. Douglas said, "We own our home in Altus and we want to take our belongings back there. They are stored in Beverly's garage. We will appreciate it if you would take us there."

Sheriff Ridden said, "That's not a problem."

Mrs. Douglas said, "We want Teri to ride back with you all. We will load up this evening and leave early in the morning."

Mr. Douglas said, "I think we had better knock out that wall to the bedroom next to Teri's room. That way it will be able to easily accommodate Triplets."

Teri said, "Dad you are the best. Keri and Jeri will be able to spend time with me at home and I can spend time with them at home."

Dianne said, "That's a great idea because we won't be able to separate them now. They have a lot to catch up on."

Mr. Douglas said, "The house with the blue trim is Beverly's home. We thank you all again. Teri we will talk with you later. We have a couple of things to do. We will let you know when we get home. We love you."

Mrs. Douglas said, "Girls give me a hug. I love all of you."

After they left the Douglas', Dianne said, "Let's go by and visit the family. They are waiting to meet Teri. Then we will go to my place."

When they got to Dianne's family home, they parked and went in. Everyone was so excited to see the Triplets together. They gathered around them and greeted Teri. She was very happy to meet more family members. They were there for about three hours. Dianne's Mom, and other family members had fixed a big dinner. An hour after they had eaten Dianne thought they should head to her place.

Dianne said, "OK everybody, it's time for us to head for my place before dark. We have had a long day."

Mr. Johnson said, "John, we appreciate you looking after our girls. We want to see more of you."

Sheriff Ridden said, "You will. It was nice seeing you all again. It reminds me of old times."

Everyone hugged and said their good-byes. Sheriff Ridden, Dianne and the girls loaded up and went to Dianne's place. When they got inside Dianne looked around very slowly. She was thinking, "Walter, I have brought your Triplets home so you can see them together. I am about to start a new life, but you will always be in my heart."

Dianne felt sadness but yet she was happy.   It was a moment that she wished Walter was still alive where he could have seen his girls.

Dianne said, "I am going to pack a few things to take back with me. Tomorrow, I will start looking for me a place."

The Triplets said, "You can get a place in our complex."

Dianne said, "No thank you. You all are grown and need your private space. You don't need your, mom looking out to see what time you come in from a date, etc."

Sheriff Ridden asked, "Are you serious? You are moving to Chillicothe?"

Dianne said, "Yes, I am serious and it's time for me to start living again. I will keep this place for a while. It's paid off so when any of us come to Dallas, we can stay here. I will get everyone a key made. This will be our hotel."

Sheriff Ridden said, "You are serious!"

Dianne said, "I can be happy there because the people I love most, are there. Now I realize that it's time for me to move on, live and be happy. Now I can start enjoying life again."

Sheriff Ridden said, "I am very happy to hear that."

The Triplets were all giggly and happy that Dianne was finally going to move to Chillicothe. Sheriff Ridden was just as happy as the girls.

Keri asked, "Why don't we sleep in the mobile home tonight? It will seem like we camped out."

Jeri and Teri asked, "Is it ok Sheriff Ridden and mom? That sounds like fun."

Sheriff Ridden looked at Dianne and she looked at him and they said, "Why not!"

They helped Dianne pack some of her personal belongings and went to the mobile home.

Sheriff Riddens' mobile home could sleep up to eight people comfortably. He slept in the front. The girls and Dianne put on their cotton pajamas. They played some cards and bingo before going to bed. It was like one big happy family. Sheriff Ridden was thinking, "This is what I have always wanted, a family. I wonder if Dianne realizes that I am in love with her. She is a beautiful and sweet person."

Dianne was thinking, "This is what I didn't get a chance to enjoy with Walter. Maybe I will get to do this with John. He seems so happy when he is with me. I know that I am happy when I am with him."

Sheriff Ridden said, "We have had a long day. I think we need to turn in so we can beat the morning traffic."

The Triplets said, "Good night, Sheriff Ridden. Good night, mom."

Sheriff Ridden said, "Good, night ladies. I will see you all in the morning."

Dianne said, "Good, night John. Thank you again, for being here for me. Good night, girls."

Sheriff Ridden said, "No problem. See you in the morning."

They all turned in and went to bed with smiles on their faces. Everybody was happy! The Triplets were happy because now they were whole. Now they can live the Triplet life. Dianne was happy because she was with John. There is no competition, or anyone to get in the way of them getting together. She has loved him since the first day, that she saw him in high school.

John Ridden was the most excited, because now he can talk to Dianne. He fell in love with her, while they were in high school, but did not have the nerve to tell her. Now she is all his. After they get home he will start, courting her. He missed out on twenty years and don't plan to lose another minute of being with her. He has silently loved her all of these years.

CHAPTER 6

Dianne Moves to Chillicothe

The next morning, the sun was shining bright and beautiful. Dianne got up first. She wanted to be dressed and have her hair combed before Sheriff Ridden saw her. She started cooking breakfast, so they could eat before they got on the highway.

Sheriff Ridden came in the kitchen area.

He said, "That smells good."

Dianne said, "Thank you. I thought we would eat before getting on the road."

By now, the Triplets were up and dressed. It seems that no matter how sleepy a person is, they can smell food and wake up.

Sheriff Ridden asked, "Did you ladies sleep well?"

"Yes Sir," they answered in unison. "Thank you."

Dianne served the crew. Thirty minutes later they were finished and the Triplets cleaned up everything. Dianne and Sheriff Ridden were up front in the captain seats.

Keri said, "I think Sheriff Ridden likes mom a lot."

Jeri said, "She said they knew each other in high school and used to hang out together."

Teri said, "The best part, I think mom likes him as much."

Keri said, "We love Sheriff Ridden. He would make a good Dad."

Jeri said, "A Dad! We didn't get to see our dad. It will would be nice to have him for our dad."

Teri said, "I have a very good dad and Sheriff Ridden reminds me of him in some ways. He is very considerate and kind."

Keri said, "I don't think that I would want anyone else to be our dad. Sheriff Ridden is nice and special."

Jeri said, "Yes, he is very special. He has been watching out for us since we met him."

Teri said, "I wouldn't mind him being my third dad."

Keri said, "Jeri and I and the rest of the family, have been trying to get mom to start dating, but she refused. Maybe God had Sheriff Ridden waiting for her."

Teri said, "It looks that way. It's like my kidnapping brought them together."

Jeri said, "I have always heard people say when bad things happen, some good comes out of it."

Keri said, "Yes and God does things in His own way and time."

Jeri said, "Now that mom will be living in Chillicothe, they will be able to see a lot of each other. Maybe they will start dating after she gets settled."

Keri said, "That will be the bomb. Mom, going on dates. That would be nice."

Jeri said, "Wow We don't even go on dates. Maybe we should look up, "The Organization of Multiple Births.""

Teri said, "Yes, because mom will end up married and we will be old maids."

They started laughing so loud. Dianne looked back to make sure everything was alright. They had a nice ride back home. Dianne and Sheriff Ridden quietly talked as they drove along. The girls decided that they were going to start watching them. They wanted to know if their suspicion was right. The weather was nice when they arrived in Chillicothe.

Sheriff Ridden said to Dianne, "When you get ready to look for an apartment, I would like to show you the best places. I don't want you to end up in a bad, area by yourself."

Dianne said, "John, you have done so much for

me and the girls. I don't want to take up all, of your spare time."

Sheriff Ridden said, "It's not a problem Dianne. I need to do something different beside work. I need to start living again myself."

Dianne said, "Well in that case, as soon as you have some free time, I can start looking for a place. I don't want it too close to the girls."

Sheriff Ridden said, "I will check my schedule and let you know what times I will be free this week. Joseph Alexander's trial is coming up soon."

Dianne said, "Well, we are here. Thank you again. The trip was nice and I enjoyed it."

The Triples started helping Sheriff Ridden take Dianne's things into their apartment. Dianne decided to leave most of her pictures with Walter in the condo. Since she was about to start over, she felt it was best to leave them there. She brought most of her clothes, purses, and shoes.

After they got their bags and Dianne's belongings in the apartment, Sheriff Ridden said, "I will talk with you later, Dianne. Then he said bye to the Triplets."

They said, "Bye Sheriff Ridden.

Dianne said, "I think I want to buy a home instead of renting an apartment."

The Triplets said, "Really! That would be awesome."

Jeri said, "When we get married, we can have Sunday dinners and other holiday gatherings."

Teri and Keri said, "That would be wonderful."

Dianne got the idea to buy a home, because if she and Sheriff Ridden marry, they will need a place to stay. He stays in a small apartment, since it's only him. He has been saving his money. Lately he had been thinking about living in his mobile home to save more money since

Dianne is here.

He has been thinking if they get married they could buy a home together. It would be big enough for the girls and Teri's parents to spend the night during the holidays. He thought maybe get a home with an in-law set up.

Sheriff Ridden called Dianne early the next morning before heading to the office.

Sheriff Ridden said, "Good morning sunshine."

Dianne was already up, showered and dressed. She knew that he would probably call her before he started his day.

Dianne said, "Good morning John. I was going to call you in a little while. I decided that I don't want to rent an apartment. I want to buy a home. I want a stable place for the girls so when they get married, they can bring their families home to visit."

Sheriff Ridden said, "Wow! You are full of many surprises."

Dianne said, "I am looking for permanence."

Sheriff Ridden said, "Well I hope I can help you find what you want."

Dianne said, "It doesn't take a lot to make me happy."

Sheriff Ridden asked, "What is your agenda for today?"

Dianne said, "I would like to ride around and see the different areas where homes are selling."

Sheriff Ridden said, "I have some free time right now. There is nothing going on at the office that Deputies Carlson and Ryan can't handle."

Dianne said, "John, I am beginning to feel like I am imposing too much on your time, and I don't mean to do that."

Sheriff Ridden said, "Dianne, if I were not spending my free time with you, I would be at the office looking at four walls. They laughed.

CHAPTER 7

Joseph Alexander Acquitted

It's a beautiful day, in June 2006 and Joseph Alexander goes on trial this morning. He didn't sleep last night because he was worrying about the outcome of his trial. Joseph keeps going over the day, Benjamin Alexander was found dead. He knows that he didn't purposely kill his grandfather. He knew he had hit his head on the table when he fell, but he couldn't understand how he died.

Joseph keeps thinking if only he would not have gone there, my mothers' father would be alive. He had prayed many times since his incarceration, that God would forgive him. Deputy Carson came in the office about 7:50 a.m. He went to the cell to check on Joseph.

Deputy Carson said, "Good morning Joseph. I will be taking you to the Courthouse about 8:30 a.m. I brought your clothes and breakfast."

Joseph Alexander said, "Good morning Deputy Carson. Thank you, kindly for the clothes and food."

Deputy Carlson said, "Your mom brought them to Sheriff Ridden."

Joseph Alexander said, "I thank you all for your kindness. I keep going over in my mind, that I don't understand how my, grandfather died. I realized his head hit the table but there was no blood. When I heard the lady at the door, I figured it was someone who knew him, and would come in the house, and if he was hurt, she would help him."

Deputy Carson said, "I don't want you to get your hopes up, but we have come up with some new evidence. I can't tell you about it, but it will come out in Court today. It just may be in your favor."

Joseph Alexander started crying uncontrollable.

Deputy Carlson said, "You must, pull yourself

together and get ready. We can't be late. Judge Hewitt will handle your case today. I hear he is a fair judge."

Joseph Alexander said, "If I am the cause of my grandfather's death, I don't need any fairness."

Deputy Carson said, "Don't beat yourself up too much. We all make some bad mistakes in life."

Joseph Alexander said, "I have always tried to do the right thing and no one, could have ever told me, that I would be in a situation like this."

Deputy Carson said, "I will be back in a few minutes to get you."

Joseph Alexander said, "Alright Sir."

In the meantime, Mrs. Rothchild and Ms. Stewart had already arrived at the Courthouse. Sheriff Ridden and Gloria Alexander were seated down front in the courtroom with Mrs. Brunswick. The FBI Agent came in about five minutes before Court started. He pulled Sheriff

Ridden aside and spoke with him.

FBI Agent Joe Smith told Sheriff Ridden, "There was someone else in Mr. Alexanders' home. I found finger prints in the pantry and I found a bloody bat. The prints on the bat did not match Joseph Alexander's prints. And the blood was Mr. Alexander's. On Mr. Alexander's wallet, there were two sets of prints. One was Joseph Alexander and the other prints matched a man in our data base. We quietly have an All Point Bulletin (APB) out on him."

Sheriff Ridden said, "Joe, thank you so much for doing a thorough investigation."

Joe Smith said, "I am glad I was able to help out."

The Bailiff told everyone to stand while Judge Hewitt was coming in the Courtroom. After the Judge Hewitt took his seat, the Bailiff told everyone they may be seated. Deputy Carson brought Joseph Alexander into the Courtroom. Joseph Alexander had to stand and face Judge

Hewitt. The Prosecuting Attorney read the charges against Joseph Alexander. Mrs. Stewart was put on the stand to identify Joseph Alexander as the man that she saw coming from behind Mrs. Brunswick's house.

The Defense Attorney spoke after that and let them know that another witness saw another man come from behind Mrs. Brunswick's house. He told the Judge that they have some new evidence that proves that Joseph Alexander did not kill his, Grandfather. The Courtroom got loud. Everyone was talking and looking around.

Then Judge Hewitt hit the gavel on the desk and said, "Quiet in the Courtroom."

Afterward they finished going over all the evidence and listening to Joseph Alexander's testimony of his version of what happed the day Mr. Benjamin Alexander died.

FBI Agent Joe Smith told the Judge, "I did a thorough investigation of Mr. Alexander's home. I found evidence that someone else was in the home. There were two sets of fingerprints on Mr. Alexander's wallet. One set matched Joseph Alexander and the other set matches a man in our data base. We have agents looking for him now. We didn't publicize it because we don't want to scare him off."

Judge Hewitt asked, "Is there anything conclusive to prove that Joseph Alexander did not kill his, Grandfather."

FBI Agent Joe Smith said, "There was a baseball bat covered in blood in the pantry. Joseph Alexander's finger prints were not on it, only the other suspect."

Judge Hewitt said, "We have another witness who saw another man come from the back of Mrs. Brunswick's home.

The D.A. called Mrs. Rothchild to the stand. She said, "Joseph Alexander is not the man that I saw coming from the back of Mrs. Brunswick's home. The man that I saw was heavy and older with some gray hair."

The D. A. asked Mrs. Rothchild, "Do you know what time, it was when you saw the other man."

Mrs. Rothchild said, "It was exactly 3:00 p.m. because my alarm went off for me to take my medication."

The Prosecuting Attorney told Judge Davidson that he wanted to call Ms. Stewart to the stand.

After she was sworn in, "He asked, "Is the man you saw coming from behind Mrs. Brunswick's home, in this Courtroom?"

Ms. Stewart said, "Yes. I saw Joseph Alexander, the defendant, come from behind Mrs. Brunswick's home."

"Are you sure it was the defendant?" He asked.

"Yes Sir. It was him," Ms. Stewart said.

He asked, "Did you notice the time?"

Ms. Stewart said, "Yes, it was 2:57 p.m. I was getting out of my car, and I checked my watch, because my soap opera comes on at 3:00 P.M."

The Prosecuting Attorney said, "No more questions."

The D.A. asked Judge Hewitt, "Can we postpone this trial until the FBI produce the other man?"

Judge Hewitt said, "I think that will be wise." The he asked FBI Agent Joe Smith, "Do you agree Agent Smith?"

FBI Agent Joe Smith said, "Yes Sir. I believe we will be able to capture this man within the next week."

Judge Hewitt said, "Court will resume one week from today."

Sheriff Carson took Joseph Alexander back to the jail and locked him up. Joseph Alexander was very nervous. He was wondering if the FBI Agent would be able to find that mysterious man, before his next Court date. But most of all, will it clear him of killing his, grandfather?

As Deputy Carson was taking Joseph Alexander back to jail, Joseph asked, "Deputy Carson do you think they will be able to find this other man in a week?"

Deputy Carson said, "The FBI Agents are trained in a way that no other law enforcement officers are trained. They usually always get their man."

Joseph Alexander said, "If they can prove that I am not responsible for my, grandfather's death, I will be able to sleep at night."

Deputy Carson said. "Don't give up on prayer."

Joseph Alexander said, "Thank you, Sir."

Gloria Alexander stayed another week with Mrs. Brunswick since Joseph will be going back to Court in a week. Mrs. Brunswick didn't mind. She was happy to have someone in the house with her. She and Gloria got along real well.

Gloria Alexander asked, "Mrs. Brunswick after this is all over, will it be alright for me to visit you sometime? "I would like to move here. I have wanted to find a small quiet town to move to and I believe this is it."

Mrs. Brunswick said, "I would be upset if you didn't visit me. I have enjoyed you being here. You are like the daughter that I never had. I hope you move here."

Gloria Alexander hugged Mrs. Brunswick and said, "You are like the mother that I never had. My mom was ill and passed when I was little and my dad never remarried."

Mrs. Brunswick asked, "Did he ever say why he never remarried?"

Gloria Alexander said, "No but I know, he was still in love with my mother. They were high school sweethearts."

Mrs. Brunswick said, "That's beautiful and yet it was sad. He didn't think about the important role of a woman, being in your life as a young girl."

Gloria Alexander said, "It wasn't so bad. He did

the best he could, and he loved me. He was a good Father and didn't spoil me either."

Mrs. Brunswick asked, "How did you escape that?" They laughed.

Gloria Alexander said, "He was pretty firm on most things."

The week went by real fast. In the meantime, the Triplets were getting a kick out of Dianne and Sheriff Ridden spending time together. Sheriff Ridden called Dianne every morning before he went to the office.

Sheriff Ridden asked, "Are you going to be in Court today?"

Dianne said, "Yes, I will be there. I want to know the outcome of this young man's trial."

Sheriff Ridden said, "Alright I will see you there. Bye for now."

Dianne said, "Bye for now."

FBI Agent Joe Smith called Sheriff Ridden and

said, "We got our man."

Sheriff Ridden Asked, "You actually have the man that the other finger prints, belong too?"

FBI Agent Joe Smith said, "You know we don't play around. We set a trap for him last night."

Sheriff Ridden said, "Thank you and thank the others also. I'll see you in Court."

Mrs. Brunswick and Gloria Alexander came in the Court ahead of Sheriff Ridden. Dianne came in shortly afterwards. When Sheriff Ridden saw Gloria Alexander and Mrs. Brunswick, he went and greeted them. As soon as he turned around, in walked the love of his life, Dianne. He went over to her right away.

Deputy Ryan brought Joseph Alexander to the Court House, and FBI Agent Joe Smith, brought the other suspect Fletcher Greenburg. When FBI Agent Joe Smith, brought Fletcher Greenburg in the Courtroom:

Mrs. Rothchild, said, "That's him, the man that I

saw coming from behind Mrs. Brunswick's home."

Judge Hewett hammered the gavel and said, "Order in the Court."

After Fletcher Greenburg was put on the stand. He confessed that he had hit Mr. Alexander on the head, took the rest of his money out of his wallet, after Joseph had left out of his home.

Fletcher Greenburg said, "I heard a lady coming in the house and she was saying," Mr. are you alright?" I stepped back inside the pantry because I didn't want the other man to see me. After the young lady checked that man, she left. I put the bat in a deep corner in the pantry and I took the money out of that man's wallet and threw it on the floor. Then I went out the backdoor and went through the fence in the other yard."

After the Judge heard everything, he announced that Joseph was acquitted for killing, Benjamin Alexander.

Judge Hewitt said, "Joseph Alexander, if your mother want to press charged against you for stealing from her father, she can do that. You are free of charges for killing Mr. Benjamin Alexander. All charges for murder are dropped against you."

Gloria and Joseph Alexander broke down in tears. Joseph Alexander fell to his knees and raised his hands praising and thanking God. Most everyone in the courthouse had tears running down their cheeks. Joseph was so thankful that he wasn't responsible for his, grandfather's death. If he were, he knew that he would have to live with it for the rest of his life.

That was his mothers' father and he didn't want that burden. He realizes that he has to be careful of choices that he makes from now on. One error can not only ruin your life but the lives of a whole family. Gloria Alexander went to her son and threw her arms around him. This was excitement, this little town had not seen in years. Everyone was happy with the outcome because they paid attention to Joseph Alexander. They could tell that he was remorseful and that he had good manners. After Gloria Alexander came to town, the citizens had empathy for her as a other. She was a very well-liked person and was very nice.

Before leaving the Courtroom, Joseph Alexander spoke to the Judge Hewitt and all the people in the courtroom. He apologized for his error and for putting his, mother through that trauma. He thanked Judge Hewitt, Sheriff Ridden, Deputies Carson, Ryan and Mrs. Brunswick for letting his, Mom stay with her. And lastly, he thanked God for hearing the prayers that were prayed for him.

Gloria Alexander told Mrs. Brunswick, "Since I work from home, it won't be a problem to move here. We will go home and settle some things and then we will be back."

Mrs. Brunswick said, "Just let me know, if you

need any kind of help. I am here for you."

Joseph Alexander spoke with Sheriff Ridden, "Sir my, Mother and I will be moving here after we go home and settle some things. I want to know, if it is at all possible for me to get a job working for you or in your office. I am very good at clerical work, phones and I learn very fast."

Sheriff Ridden said, "I can't make any promises right now but after you get back, I will see what I can do for you."

Joseph Alexander said, "Thank you, Sir! Thank You!"

Sheriff Ridden said, "If I can't get you anything here, I have a Sheriff friend in Altus who may have something. After you get back, I will see what we can do to help you. It's only fifteen minutes from here."

Joseph Alexander said, "I won't let you down, Sir. Thank you again."

Gloria and Mrs. Brunswick said their good-byes.

She made sure that she thanked, Sheriff Ridden and Deputies Carson and Ryan before she left also.

Sheriff Ridden went to Dianne and asked, "Are you hungry? I thought you might like to get something to eat before going home. This way, I won't have to eat alone," he said.

Dianne said, "Well, we certainly don't want you eating alone."

They laughed and walked out of the Courtroom and went to the local diner. Sheriff Ridden was thinking how nice it is to have Dianne living in Chillicothe now. He realizes that sooner or later he will need to tell her how he felt about her from the first day that they met.

Dianne has been so happy since she moved to Chillicothe, and she is much happier when she is with Sheriff Ridden. Her thoughts, "Maybe dad will get his wish after all."

Over the years when she thought about John

Ridden. She always remembered her father saying, that he hoped they would have gotten together. John Ridden was a well-mannered young man and always respected others.

In high school his friends loved him because he was special. If he could help a person he would and was very sincere. Dianne loved him but didn't have the nerve to give him a hint. After her best friend Denise put a claim on him, that broke her heart. Then she did everything she could to keep her mind off of him.

CHAPTER 8

Sheriff Ridden and Dianne Dates

Since Dianne made her decision to move to Chillicothe, she has not stopped smiling. She and Sheriff Ridden spend all of their spare time together. The Organization of Multi Births of America were found by the Triplets. Their goal was to meet male Identical Triplets, within their age range and no more than 4 years older.

Sheriff Ridden figures now that Dianne has gotten settled in this last two months, that it's time to let her know that he wants to court her.

Sheriff Ridden called Dianne.

Ring! Ring! Dianne answered, "Hello John."

Sheriff Ridden loves the way she answers his calls. He said, "Hi Dianne. I am calling to invite you out Friday night, if you are free."

Dianne said, "Well, I guess I will need to check,

my calendar, and get back with you on that."

Sheriff Ridden was surprised at her answer. He wasn't sure what to think. He was very quiet.

Dianne asked, "John, are you still there?"

Sheriff Ridden said, "I am here." He was a little nervous now.

Dianne asked, "Is anything special happening?"

Sheriff Ridden said, "Well yes! I am asking you out on a date and I have a special place, that I would like to take you."

Dianne was quiet now. She is about to get her wish.

Sheriff Ridden asked, "Are you there Dianne?"

Dianne answered, "Yes, I am here. Then she asked, "What's a good time for me to be ready and how should I dress?"

Sheriff Ridden said, "I will pick you up at 7:45 p.m. and dressy casual. I will be wearing a black and tan tie, black Jacket, black slacks and a tan shirt and black shoes."

Dianne said, "Wow! I just might be able to accommodate you. I will see what I can do."

Sheriff Ridden said, "Alright, I will see you then. Bye."

Dianne said, "Alright. Bye."

Dianne was in her room when the Sheriff called. She ran into the living room and said, "Girls!"

All three of them were asking, "What's wrong Mom?"

Dianne sat down calmly and said, "Sheriff Ridden just asked me out on a date. We will be dressy casual, he said."

The Triplets were jumping up and down, "We knew it."

"Mom, we are going to hook you up. We are going to give you a make-over," the Triplets said. "You are going to knock him off his feet."

Dianne said, "Slow down. Sit down. There is something that I need to tell you guys. John doesn't know this but I must tell you all."

All three of them held up their fingers.

Dianne said, "Just let me tell you all this, and I don't think you will have many questions afterwards. Years ago in high school, the first day that I saw John Ridden, I fell in love with him. He never seemed to notice me in that way. He began to hang out with me and my friend Denise and some more kids. Soon Denise put a claim on him. She started calling him her boyfriend but he never said anything. So I tried to stop thinking about him in that way. When we graduated, I went to California to go to College and get away from him. After two and a half years, they got married. And we lost contact after that."

The Triplets fingers were up again.

Dianne said, "Teri, your hand went up first and I will let you all talk in order of when you put up your fingers."

Teri said, "Why didn't you say something back then?"

Dianne said, "When I was growing up, girls didn't approach boys. It was proper etiquette for him to make the first move."

Keri said, "This is very interesting."

Jeri said. "That's what I was going to say. Continue Mom."

Dianne said, "A lot of boys tried to hit on me, but I ignored them and stayed focused on school. When I met Walter, it was almost like he was John. They had ways alike, very polite and considerate and I fell in love with him. My dad always told me, that he thought John was going to be his son-in-law. When John showed up at my door, I could not believe it. When I found out that his wife Denise had passed, I was hurt because she was my best friend. After he told me how selfish she was, despite of what he did to try and please her, she wasn't satisfied. I was angry at myself."

Jeri asked, "Where are you all going?"

Dianne said, "I don't know, but he said he will be wearing black pants, black jacket, tan/black tie and a tan shirt and black shoes."

Keri said, "Mom, we are going to match you with his colors. We are going to hook you up and make you so beautiful, you are going to scare yourself."

Teri said, "That's right. Your make-up is going be natural and you are going to shine."

Jeri said, "Mom, Sheriff Ridden may not ever want you out his sight again."

They all laughed. Dianne is happy that she has the Triplets to share this moment with her. The Triplets are so excited. They took Dianne into her room, to look for a very special outfit, that will match Sheriff Riddens' clothes. Dianne is getting nervous. It has been over twenty years, since she went on a date. Now that her date is with John Ridden, it's extra special. After going through Dianne's clothes, the Triplets decided that they needed to take her shopping.

Keri said, "Mom, you need a sexy outfit. You need something that will bring your beauty out."

Jeri said, "We need to find an outfit that will show your beautiful curves."

Teri said, "I know the exact place to take you. Let's go girls."

They got in the car and went to a Boutique, not far from their home. When they got there and went in, Keri and Jeri said, "This is it."

Teri said, "Mom sit here. We will be back with just what you need."

The Triples left Dianne and they went and found three outfits for her to try on. When they brought her the outfits, they said, "Come on to the dressing room."

Dianne got up and followed them. When she tried on the first outfit, it was ok. But when she came out in the second outfit, the Triplets said, "That's it!"

It was a tight-fitting black dress with thin tan long sleeves and in the center of the dress was a v strip of tan and then a black v strip above that one. The dress looked like it was made for Dianne's figure. After the girls paid for Dianne's outfit, they rushed her home. She had some dangling tan earrings and a beautiful black bracelet with little hearts on it.

The Triplets noticed that Dianne was still wearing her wedding rings. They looked at each other and all three of them put their fingers up. Dianne looked at them in wonderment.

Then she asked, "What's wrong?"

They said, "You cannot go on a date, wearing your wedding rings. They must come off."

Dianne said, "Wow! I have had them on so long,

I never thought about them. Thank you, guys for being so observant."

Dianne sat on the bed looking at her rings. Slowly she took them off. Her eyes watered.

Keri said, "Mom, it's going to be alright."

They all hugged her. Then she got up and put her rings in her jewelry box.

Jeri said, "After you take your shower, we will put on your make-up. We need to get moving. You don't ever want to rush make-up."

Dianne said, "Alright ladies. I am going to take my shower and I will let you all know when I am finished."

When Dianne finished showering, she called the girls in the bedroom. They were so excited that their mom was finally going, on a date. The Triplets put make-up on Dianne, and helped her put her dress on where she didn't mess up her make-up. Then they put a towel around her shoulders so they could do her hair.

They rolled her long, beautiful hair into curls and pinned it. When they finished you would have thought that she went to the beauty salon. It was time for Sheriff Ridden to show up. When the doorbell rang, Teri said, "I will get it."

When she opened the door, Sheriff Ridden said, "Good evening." He wasn't sure which Triplet it was.

Teri said, "Good evening Sheriff Ridden. Come in and have a seat. Mom will be out in a few minutes."

In about three minutes Keri and Jeri accompanied Dianne into the living room. When Sheriff Ridden saw Dianne, he almost fell over. He had never seen her looking so beautiful before.

Dianne said, "Hello John."

Sheriff Ridden said, "Hel-lo Dianne. You look awesome"

Dianne said, "You look pretty good yourself."

Sheriff Ridden asked, "Shall we go now?"

Dianne said, "Girls don't wait up for me and lock the door."

The Triplets said, "You all have fun and be safe."

Sheriff Ridden held up his arm for Dianne to take it as they walked to the car. He opened the car door for her and closed it after she got in the car. He was always a gentleman but this was very special.

Dianne said, 'Thank you, John."

He went to the driver's side and got in. He turned to Dianne and just stared at her.

Dianne asked, "John is anything wrong?"

Sheriff Ridden said, "No. I have always known that you were beautiful, but tonight you are breathtaking."

Dianne said, "Thank you, John. That's quite a compliment."

Sheriff Ridden said, "It fits, believe me."

They rode in silence until they got to the restaurant. Sheriff Ridden took Dianne to a nice new place about forty minutes from Chillicothe. They had a nice band and it was beautifully decorated. When they walked in the door, all eyes were on them. This place had a nice dance floor also. They were shown to a table closer to the front, where the band was playing.

Sheriff John Ridden had requested a couple of songs, that were popular when they were in school. Of course they were slow songs. He wanted to hold Dianne close tonight. He had wanted to do that for a long time. Neither one of them drank liquor so they drank tea. When the band played one of the songs from their past, Sheriff Ridden got up and walked over to Dianne.

Sheriff Ridden asked, "May I have this dance?"

Dianne put her hand in his and said, "Yes you may."

They started dancing. Dianne could feel Sheriff Riddens' body trembling. She was a little nervous too. After a few minutes they both relaxed and enjoyed their dance. After Dinner they sat and talked. They did not want the night to end. But they had one more dance before they left.

Dianne said, "John, thank you for a wonderful evening. This is a very nice place."

Sheriff Ridden said, "Thank you for a beautiful evening. I can't remember when I enjoyed myself more. I guess we should head for home."

Dianne said, "It's a true saying, "When you are having fun, the time seems to fly."

Sheriff Ridden said, "That is very true."

When he brought Dianne home, of course the Triplets were still up and waiting for her. He walked her to the front door, took her key and unlocked the door. Then he kissed her on the forehead and said, "Good night, Dianne."

Dianne said, "Good night, John."

As soon as Dianne stepped inside the apartment, the lights came on and the Triplets were shouting, "Tell us about your date." They were laughing and hugging Dianne.

Sheriff Ridden could barely think straight driving fifteen minutes to his place. He kept thinking how he felt, when he first met Dianne, but didn't have the nerve to approach her. Tonight, he knows, that he has been in love with her, all of these years.

Now the Sheriff and Dianne spend all of their free time together. Sometimes they just went riding. They really enjoy each other's company. Two months later Sheriff Ridden felt it was time for him to come clean and tell Dianne how he felt. They had gone to a movie and stopped on the way home at the drive-up eatery. They were sitting there just talking about little things. Finally, Sheriff Ridden turned to Dianne.

Dianne asked, "Are you all right John?"

Sheriff Ridden said, "I am fine, but there is something that I need to tell you. I should have told you over twenty years ago."

Dianne said, "John, you sound so serious." Then she asked, "You are not sick or anything like that, are you?"

Sheriff Ridden ask, "Dianne do you remember the first day that we met? You had on a black fitted skirt and a pink blouse."

Dianne said, "What a memory. I remember and you were wearing nice pressed jeans and a white t-shirt and some blue and white tennis."

Sheriff Ridden said, "I am not the only one with a good memory. Dianne, I fell in love with you that day and I have loved you ever since."

Dianne said, "John!"

Sheriff Ridden said, "Please let me finished while I can. I only started hanging around you and Denise and the others, so I could be close to you. When Denise started telling everyone that

I was her boyfriend, I didn't want to embarrass her by denying it. After you went to California to College, I almost died. Since you weren't dating anyone, I thought you would probably turn me down. So I never got the nerve to ask you out."

Dianne asked, "John Ridden, remember when you came to Dallas, to tell me about my baby being alive? We were talking and I told you that I was in love with a guy, but he didn't know I was alive? You were the guy. You see, I fell in love with you the first day that I saw you. After Denise started saying you were her boyfriend, then I focused on my studies, to keep from thinking about you. When I met Walter, it was like you in another body. His demeanor and everything was you and I fell in love with him."

Sheriff Ridden said, "You are serious! When I told you in Dallas that I was in love with a girl who didn't know I existed, I almost told you that evening."

Dianne said, "Very much so. John that's why it

was easy for me to spend so much time with you. That's why I decided to move to Chillicothe, so I could be close to you also."

Sheriff Ridden and Dianne had tears in their eyes now. He looked at Dianne and asked, "May I kiss you?"

Dianne said, "You don't have to ask."

They embraced each other with a long passionate kiss that left them shaking. They were hugging, laughing and kissing. They could not believe that they both, felt the same way and didn't know how to let it be known.

Sheriff Ridden said, "I didn't date anyone. I just ended up marrying Denise because she was there. After her death, I never even thought about dating anyone else. All I could think about was the chance that I missed with you."

Dianne said, "I didn't date when I was in school because I had fell in love with you. After Walter passed, I didn't want to date again. You were so deep my heart, that I didn't want to date anyone else. My family and the girls kept trying to push me to date. How could I tell them that I was in love with a man who didn't know that I was in love with him."

Sheriff Ridden said, "When God has someone for you, it will work out. I know He had us for each other. Look at the way we found each other. Only God could orchestrate that."

Dianne said, "I am a believer. I know He works miracles. The day you showed up at my door, I knew He sent you."

Sheriff Ridden said, "That day when I looked at the twins video for the second time, I saw you in it and almost fainted. I couldn't wait to see you. I didn't know what would happen, but I knew I had to come in person. You looked as if you had not aged. I just couldn't believe I found you. It's getting late I had better get you home."

Dianne said, "We have a lot of catching up to do. One other thing, you know my daughters, and we will have all three of their approval, with no problems. How great is that?" She asked.

Sheriff Ridden said, "I love them, and they love me. We are already family. I loved you, Dianne Johnson from the first day that I met you."

Dianne said, "I love you John Ridden. I always have and always will."

Sheriff Ridden brought Dianne home and walked her to her door. After he unlocked her door, he kissed her for a long time. He didn't want to let her go. They have confessed their love for each other, and now it's going to be hard, for them to be apart.

The Triplets were still up waiting to find out how their evening went. When they saw Dianne's face, they knew it went very well. She was glowing and her smile was from ear to ear.

Keri said, "I don't think we need to ask anything. Let's go to bed and let Mom, keep reminiscing about her evening. She can tell us about it in the morning."

Teri and Jeri said, "Good idea. We don't want to spoil her memories."

They started laughing and the Triplets went to their room. Dianne went to her room and stood in front of her mirror. She could not believe what had happened tonight. All these years, she had no idea that John Ridden was in love with her, and he had no idea that she was in love with him.

Dianne took a shower and put on her night clothes and lay on her bed. She was engrossed in her thoughts of the evening, "John Ridden and I hugged and kissed each other. We professed our love for each other. I can't believe it!" Finally, she fell asleep.

The next morning, the Triplets were waiting for her when she came out of her room. Dianne had the biggest smile on her face.

Dianne said, "Good morning darlings!"

The Triplets said, "Good morning, Mom."

They had breakfast ready so they all went to the table and sat down, looking at Dianne.

Dianne asked, "Is something wrong?"

Their response was, "No Mom."

After they finished eating, Dianne said, "I know you guys are waiting to hear about my evening. Let's go to the living room."

The Triplets jumped up and rushed in and sat down, all looking at Dianne. She started laughing at them.

Dianne said, "You guys are funny. I wish you could see yourselves."

They laughed! Dianne began to tell them about her evening. She told them how she felt about John Ridden the first time she saw him.

Dianne said, "Last night, John told me that he fell in love with me the first day he laid eyes on me. He even remembered the clothes that I had on. He said he has been in love with me all of these years. And I had to come clean and tell him, that was why I didn't date after Walter died. I was in love with him and didn't want to be with anyone else. He told me the only reason he married Denise was because I had left town without saying good-bye. He married her two and a half years after I went to California. He said after she passed, he didn't date because he didn't want to be with anyone else. He said he could not get me out of his heart or mind."

The Triplets held up their fingers to speak.

Dianne said, "Jeri, first, Teri second and then Keri."

Jeri asked, "Mom how did you feel when Sheriff Ridden showed up at your door in Dallas?"

Dianne said, "I had mixed emotions but I was very glad it was him. I knew only God could have sent him."

Teri asked, "Were you nervous, when you saw

him."

Dianne said, "Actually I was too excited to be nervous. I could hardly believe my eyes. But one thing always fascinated me, was that my, Dad told me several times, that he always thought John would be his son-in-law."

Keri said, "He probably could tell you guy were in love with each other, when he was with the both of you."

Dianne said, "I don't know, but I thought John didn't have a thought about me. Boy, was I wrong! Well, we have confessed how we feel about each other. I even told him what clothes he was wearing, and the shoes he had on the first day that I saw him."

Jeri said, "This is so interesting and now look, how we met Sheriff Ridden and became friends with him and didn't know he was in love with our mother."

Keri said, "Life is full of strange events. You just

never know what to expect."

Teri asked, "What's next? A wedding?"

Dianne said, "We are really just getting to know each other in a different way. We will know when it's time. We will be in prayer about our relationship and you all in this relationship."

The phone rang. Ring! Ring! Ring!

Dianne said, "I will get it. She picked up and said, "Good morning darling!"

The Triplets burst out laughing. They excused themselves from the room.

Sheriff Ridden said, "Good morning my love. I couldn't sleep last night. I wanted to kiss you over and over."

Dianne said, "I can't wait to see you. She asked, "When will you be free?"

Sheriff Ridden said, "I have some things to finish up here in the office. Meet me for lunch at Lola's."

Dianne said, "I will see you then. I love you. Bye"

Sheriff Ridden said, "O.k. I love you more. Later."

Sheriff Ridden is already thinking about buying an engagement ring for Dianne. He plans to get it before the week is over. They have waited over twenty years and there is no need to keep waiting. He has been in love with her, all of this time and he knows it will never change.

They met for lunch and were like two teenagers discovering love. They sat next to each other. Normally they sat across from each other. After they finished lunch, Sheriff Ridden walked Dianne to her car.

He kissed her on the cheek and said, "I will see you later."

Dianne said, "Later and got in her car and went home."

On the way home Dianne had butterflies in her

stomach. She just couldn't believe it. She finally had her man. There were some other things Sheriff Ridden had to take care of in the office, so he and Dianne didn't get to see each other for two days. This was hard for both of them. They had gotten used to spending all of their spare time together. Finally they were able to make a date for Friday night.

Sheriff Ridden took Dianne out to dinner but brought her home early.

Dianne asked, "John is anything wrong?"

Sheriff Ridden said, "No, I haven't seen the Triplets in a while. I would like to stop in and talk with them for a few minutes."

Dianne said, "They will love that. They talk about you all of the time. You are their hero."

When they got to Dianne's place, before they went inside, Sheriff Ridden stole him a kiss. They giggled and went inside.

The Triples were sitting around, but when they

saw Sheriff Ridden they got up and said, "Hello Sheriff Ridden."

Sheriff Ridden said, "Hello ladies. It's been a while since I have seen you all."

The Triplets said, "We have missed you too."

Sheriff Ridden said, "I would like to talk to all of you for a few minutes."

The Triplets sat on the couch. Sheriff Ridden held out his hand to Dianne. She reached for his hand and walked closer to him.

Sheriff Ridden said, "You all know that Dianne and have been spending a lot of time together. But what you probably don't know, is that I have been in love with her since high school. I have known Keri and Jeri long before I knew she were their mother. Teri and I met after Mr. Benjamin Alexander was killed. What I am trying to say is, as he was pulling out a ring box out of his pocket, I am her today to ask you all for your mothers' hand in marriage."

The Triplets started screaming. Dianne started crying. Sheriff Ridden got on one knee in front of Dianne.

Sheriff Ridden said, "Dianne, I have been in love with you, since the first day that I laid eyes on you. I loved you then and I have loved you, all of the past years, and I will love you forever. I am asking you to accept my offer to be my wife?"

The Triplets said, "Yes! Yes!"

Dianne fell in Sheriff Riddens' arms and said, "Yes John. I have loved you all these years and will love you forever."

They kissed and the Triplets were jumping up and down with joy.

Sheriff Ridden said, "I almost forgot. I have something for you guys. He pulled out three more ring boxes. I won't only be marrying your mother, but I will be marrying you all, too."

He put a ring on each one of the Triplets fingers and kissed them on their cheeks.

Sheriff Ridden said, "We are now family. Dianne, we have waited long enough. We need to let our families know, that we have found each other and set a wedding date."

The Triplets were crazy with excitement. They were happy that Sheriff Ridden was in love with their mom, and that he would be their Dad.

After everybody settled down Dianne said, "We can call our families tomorrow and give them the news."

For years Dianne's family had been trying to get her to start dating but she refused. She knew where her heart was even though she didn't know where John Ridden was.

CHAPTER 9

Dianne Calls the Douglas'

The Douglas' moved back into their home in Altus. They were constantly thanking God for not having to go to prison. The main thing they were worried about was leaving Teri behind. Since Dianne spoke on their behalf in the Courtroom, the Judge had mercy on them. Mr. Douglas was extending Teri's room so when Keri and Jeri spent time with them, the room would be big enough for all three of them.

Now that they are an extended family, they will share a lot of family time together. Right now, Teri is staying with her sisters and their mom which is her biological mom also. Now the Triplets have two moms and is about to have a third dad, even though they didn't get to know their biological Dad. He was killed in a car accident a couple of hours before they were born. Now people will no longer know Keri and

Jeri as twins. Since they have found their Identical Triplet alive, they will be the Identical Triplets. Teri was stolen as a baby at the hospital, where they were born. The head Nurse Beverly had stolen her and given Teri to her sister Megan and brother-in-law Robert. She told Dianne that Teri had died from respiratory problems.

The Triplets are headed toward their twenty first birthday. Now that Sheriff Ridden and Dianne are engaged to be married, they are going to have their mothers plan their wedding in Chillicothe, Texas. Since Dianne married Walter in Dallas and John Ridden married Denise in Dallas, they want to keep that separated and marry in Chillicothe. It's June 2006 and they want their wedding to be on August 30, 2006. Dianne and Sheriff Ridden were talking about looking for a home to buy together.

Dianne decided to call Megan Douglas to make arrangements where they could spend, some family time together with the Triplets. Teri last saw them in the Courtroom when they were put on probation. She has been busy getting to know her biological mom, Dianne and her two Identical Triplet Sisters.

The phone rang at the Douglas' home. Ring! Ring!

Megan answered, "Hello."

Dianne said, "Hi this is Dianne Johnson."

Megan said, "Hi Mrs. Johnson. Is everything alright?"

Dianne said, "First, call me Dianne please. Everything and Teri are fine."

Megan said, "Thank you, and I am Megan."

Dianne said, "Well Megan, I am calling so we can figure out a day and time, where we all can get some family time together. We need to start having gatherings, so we can get to know each other, and the Triplets can get used to having, two families."

Megan said, "That sounds like a wonderful idea. Dianne, my husband and I will never be able to thank you, for speaking on our behalf in Court. We know we did a terrible wrong and now we have to forgive ourselves."

Dianne said, "Megan even though we sometimes do a wrong, God makes some good out of it. I am so thankful that you all took good care of my baby. That was a blessing for me."

Megan said, "Dianne, we love her so much. We had been trying so hard to get pregnant. Robert and I have been thanking God for letting you, be the person that you are. I sincerely thank you for reaching out to us, so we can start being family."

Dianne said, "Megan, I figure it will be better for all of us, to love each other and get along rather than bickering. It takes so much energy to bicker than it does to love. That wouldn't be good for us or the girls either."

Megan said, "Dianne, I love you already. We are going to be fine."

Dianne said, "The same here. God already has it worked out. Talk with your husband and I will talk with the girls, so we can get together soon. Bye for now."

Megan said, "Ok I will talk with Robert. Bye."

After Dianne got off the phone with Megan Douglas, she called Sheriff Ridden. He was at the office, but she called his cell phone, because it was a private call.

Sheriff Riddens' cell phone rang. He answered and said, "Hello my love."

Dianne said, "Hello Darling. She asked, "How are you?"

Sheriff Ridden said, "I am on cloud nine. I love you so much Dianne."

Dianne said, "I love you too. I am so happy. I just wanted to hear your voice. Call me when you have some free time. Oh, I called Megan Douglas, so we can work out a day and time, so we all can spend some time together."

Sheriff Ridden said, "That sounds wonderful. You all need to get to know each other because of Teri."

Dianne said, "That includes you too, you know. You will be her third dad."

They laughed and Sheriff Ridden said, "Yes ma'am. I have a call coming in. Love you. Bye."

Dianne said, "Love you too. Bye."

Dianne decided to call her, mom and dad and break the news to them. Mr. and Mrs. Johnson had finished their breakfast and were watching a morning game show. Their phone rang. Ring! Ring! Mrs. Johnson got up and answered the phone.

Mrs. Johnson said, "Hello."

Dianne said, "Hello lovely lady. I love you very

much." She asked, "Are you and dad busy? Is he in the house?"

Mrs. Johnson asked, "Is everything alright honey?"

Dianne said, "Yes mom, I want you to put on the speaker so dad can hear me."

Mrs. Johnson walked over to the couch and sat next to Mr. Johnson. She said, "Alright Dianne, we can hear you."

Dianne said, "Mom, Dad last night John Ridden proposed to me and the Triplets."

Mr. Johnson jumped up and said, "I told you that he was supposed to be my son-in-law!"

Mr. Johnson was so excited that he was dancing all over the room and saying, "I told you! I told you!"

Mrs. Johnson said, "Honey, I am so happy for you all. Your dad is dancing all over the room."

Dianne said, "John and I are going to marry here

in Chillicothe and we want his mother and you to plan the wedding. He will call his Parents today. I told him to give his mother your phone number."

Mrs. Johnson said, "Ok honey." She asked, "What date do you have in mind."

Dianne said, "August 30, 2006 and she started laughing."

Mrs. Johnson said, "Wow! In two months!"

Dianne said, "We don't want to wait. We have wasted a lot of years."

Mr. Johnson said, "You sure have. If you would have listened to me over twenty years ago, you would still be married."

Dianne said, "I know dad but we wouldn't have the Triplets. John proposed to them and gave each one of them a ring. He told them, "We are family. Well, I have to go for now. Love y'all."

Mr. Johnson said, "We happy and love you."

CHAPTER 10

THE WEDDING

They are already in the month of June. Mrs. Ridden and Mrs. Johnson realize that they need to put on their roller skates. First, they need to find out what colors, the bride and groom want to dress in and how many guests, they are inviting to their wedding.

Mrs. Barbara Ridden called Mrs. Johnson. The phone rang.

Ring! Ring! Mrs. Francis Johnson answered with, "Hello."

Mrs. Ridden said, "Hi Francis. It's been a while since we spoke or seen each other. Where does the time go?"

Mrs. Johnson said, "Hi Barbara! It's great to hear your voice. Girl, we will be in wheel chairs before we know it. Time is like a 747 jet!" They laughed.

Mrs. Ridden said, "John called me a few minutes ago with the good news. We wondered what took him so long. He has been in love with Dianne since high school."

Mrs. Johnson said, "Eric has always told Dianne that John was supposed to be his son-in-law. Honey, when he heard the news, he got up dancing all over the room. He kept saying over and over, "I told you! I told you!"

Mrs. Ridden said, "We know we can't ask for a better person than Dianne, to be our daughter-in-law. That other thang he married was from I don't know where. She was never satisfied with anything, that he did to try and please her."

Mrs. Johnson said, "Well that's the way it is sometimes. We have to let them make their own choices but that's over and we are going to be family."

Mrs. Ridden said, "Yes ma'am. Now we have to get this wedding planned. Thank God. I am so happy that it's John, someone we love."

Mrs. Johnson said, "I was so excited that, I didn't think to ask about their colors or how many guests they plan to have. But she did tell me, that they are going to marry in Chillicothe."

Mrs. Ridden said, "Good! I haven't visited John there and it will be their special place. Let me know their colors and the number of guests when you find out. I have a call coming in. Bye."

Mrs. Johnson said, "OK. I will talk with you later. Bye."

Sheriff Ridden called Dianne. Her phone rang. Ring! Ring!

She answered, "Hi baby."

Sheriff Ridden said, "Hi sweetheart. I was calling to see if we all could spend the evening together."

Dianne said, "I have not heard them talking about doing anything." She asked, "That should be fine. You know they are crazy about you. And we can get the Triplet's help with the colors."

Sheriff Ridden said, "I know and I am crazy about them too. We need to let our moms know the colors, we want and how many guests we want to invite. I realize this is going to be quick, so we need to get the ball rolling."

Dianne said, "Come over when you get off work. We can order chicken wings, baked beans and potato salad for dinner. We can kick things around with the girls after we eat."

Sheriff Ridden said, "That sounds so good. I am ready to eat now." They laughed. He said, "I will be there as soon as, I am off work. Bye baby love."

Dianne said, "Bye, my love."

Dianne got the Triplets together. They were excited that Sheriff Ridden wanted them involved in their wedding plans. They decided on Black and pale yellow. Sheriff Ridden would wear a black suit with a pale-yellow shirt, black tie and a small black/pale-yellow striped scarf in his pocket and black shoes. Dianne's will wear a pale-yellow dress with one black lace strip on the dress from the waist down. Across the breast, there will be strips of black lace and the dress will be tight fitting, with a thin black train attached from the shoulders down, black shoes and dangling pale-yellow earrings. Her hair will be pinned up with a couple of curls hanging down on each side of her face, and pale-yellow shoes. This is what the Triplets came up with.

Dianne asked, "Where are you all going to find this dress, that you want me to wear?"

The Triplets said at once, "We have already found it. The store owner is holding it for us. After Sheriff Ridden proposed, we got to work looking for that perfect dress for you."

Dianne said, "Well! I guess all we need is for John to like the colors."

The Triplets said, "He is going to say, "If it's alright with Dianne, it is fine with me."

They laughed and said, "You know men are like

that."

Dianne said, "I guess we will put it to the test this evening. John will be over after work. He will be eating dinner with us. I am going to order chicken wings, baked beans and potato salad."

Keri raised her finger.

Dianne said, "Yes, Keri?'

Keri said, "Did you order something to drink?"

Jeri raised her two fingers and said, "We have some bottles of diet green tea."

Teri held up her three fingers and said, "We also have some sprite sodas."

Dianne said, "Good. If anyone wants something else, we have plenty of water."

They all laughed. When Sherriff Ridden got there, the food had arrived fifteen minutes earlier. Dianne had ordered it like that, so they wouldn't have to wait to eat, after he got there.

After they finished eating, they went into the living room and sat down. Dianne and Sheriff Ridden sat next to each other.

Dianne said, "I will let the Triples talk first since they have decided on some nice colors for us. Teri, we will start with you, then, Jeri and Keri last."

This is because Keri is usually first most of the time. Teri got up as if she was presenting an idea to a job.

"My sisters, and I started looking for a wedding dress for mom after the proposal. We found this beautiful dress that will knock you off your feet Sheriff Ridden," Teri said. "Now I will let Jeri take over."

Jeri said, "Thank you, as she got up. Well Sheriff Ridden, we decided that black and pale-yellow would be the perfect colors for you and mom. We think you should wear a black suit with a pale-yellow shirt, a black tie and small black/pale-yellow striped scarf in your coat pocket and black shoes. Now I will turn it over to Keri."

Keri gets up and said, "Thank you, Jeri. Now moms' dress is going to be the killer. She describes their moms' dress and attire. When Keri finished, she asked Sheriff Ridden, "What do you think, Sir?"

Sheriff Ridden turned to Dianne and said, "It sounds wonderful to me but whatever Dianne wants, is alright with me."

They all laughed and Dianne said, "It sounds wonderful to me. This has saved me the headache of picking colors."

Sheriff Ridden said, "Honey, we need to decide on the number of guests for our wedding?"

Dianne said, "Write down your family and friends and I will do the same. Then we will look at the ones closest to us then decide if we need to eliminate some."

Sheriff Ridden said, "I was thinking since we are about to buy a home, we could keep it kind of small. Say basically, the immediate family and one or two friends."

Dianne said, "That sounds economical to me."

Sheriff Ridden said, "Now we need to figure out which Chapel we want to use. It's only two in town."

Dianne said, "We can check them out and get their prices or maybe our daughters can handle that for us."

The Triplets are so funny. They jumped and said, "We will do that. And we will have pale-yellow and black flowers."

Dianne said, "Black flowers?"

The Triplets said, "Yes mom. We have it covered."

Sheriff Ridden and Dianne laughed and said,

"Thank y'all."

Sheriff said, "I guess I will be heading home. I've got some things in the office that I need to work on before the office open. Good night ladies."

Dianne said, "I will walk out with you."

When they got outside they talked a few minutes.

Sheriff Ridden said, "We have some wonderful daughters and laughed."

Dianne said, "We sure do.

They kissed and said, "Good night."

When Dianne went back inside, she told the Triplets to call her mom and let her know about the color scheme. She went in her room and prayed. She thanked God for bringing John back into her life. She asked if He would bless them and her daughters to be happy together as a family. She also thanked God for the time that she had with Walter and for giving her the girls.

After the Triplets called Mrs. Johnson, their grandmother and gave her their color scheme, they said would call with the guest list in a day or two.

Mrs. Johnson called Mrs. Ridden. Her phone rang. Ring! Ring!

Mrs. Ridden answered, "Hello Francis. Do you have some news?"

Mrs. Johnson said, "Hello Barbara. Yes I have the color scheme. The Triplets are going to call me in a day or two with the guest list.

Mrs. Ridden said, "Good. Once we know how many people, we can decide on what to have and how much. John told me that it wasn't going to be too big since they are about to buy a home."

Mrs. Johnson said, "Isn't that wonderful. I was thinking maybe we could have some finger foods since it's going to be small."

Mrs. Ridden said, "Finger food sound good to

me." She asked, "What do you think of cold cut sandwiches cut in fours and pizza cut in small pieces like the sandwiches, salad and punch and sprite for the drinks."

Mrs. Johnson said, "You are a quick thinker. That sounds perfect to me and they will have their wedding cake. I will run this by Dianne and see if she agrees and I will let you know. I don't think there will be a problem. Any way I will chat with you in a day or so. Bye."

Mrs. Ridden said, "I will wait for your call. Bye."

Dianne and Sheriff Ridden agreed on the finger food. The Triplets chose the Chapel. As the plans fell in place, it seemed like the time just rushed right on by. Well, it turned out that Sheriff Ridden and Dianne's guest list was only twenty people with them and their immediate families. Sheriff Ridden invited Roger Dale and his wife.

Sheriff Ridden and Dianne's Parents came up two days before the wedding. The couple did not plan for a honey moon. They had found a house in June. Sheriff Ridden didn't go inside of it. He told Dianne that he wants to carry her over the threshold after they are married. He needed her to go in to make sure it was what she wanted.

When Sheriff Riddens' family came up, they stayed in his mobile home. The Triplets stayed at Teri's Parents home and Dianne's Parents stated with her in Keri and Jeri's apartment.

When the wedding started, Dianne's Dad walked her down the aisle. The Triplets were the flower girls and Roger Dale was the ring bearer and Mr. Ridden was Sheriff Ridden's best man. Dianne's Dad walked her down the aisle. Dianne's, mother was her maid of honor. Everything was so beautiful. Dianne's dad had tears running down his cheek. Their mothers kept wiping their eyes. They were so happy for Dianne and John Ridden.

The Triplets could hardly contain themselves.

They were thinking about if their biological dad had lived. They didn't get a chance to know him. Keri and Jeri had never had a male figure in their lives as a dad because after their dad passed, Dianne did not date anyone. Now she is marrying Sheriff John Ridden. Keri and Jeri met him after they moved from Dallas, Texas, when they graduated from college. They became good friends and he always watched out for them.

They feel that they could not have had a better person to become their dad than Sheriff Ridden. He was a very nice man with great manners. He loved them and their mother.

As Mr. Johnson brought Dianne up to Sheriff Ridden, the Pastor asked who was giving Dianne away.

Her dad said, "I am not giving her away. I am getting a son."

Everyone laughed and the Pastor asked, "Is there anyone here, who objects to these two people being united in holy matrimony? Speak now or forever hold your peace."

As Sheriff John Ridden and Dianne Johnson faced each other, The Pastor asked, "John Ridden, do you take this woman, Dianne Johnson to be your lawful wedded wife, if so say, "I do."

Sheriff John Ridden said, "I do, so help me God."

The Pastor asked, "Dianne Johnson, do you take this man, John Ridden to be your lawful wedded husband, if so say, "I do."

Dianne Johnson said, "I do, so help me God."

The Pastor said, "By the law of God invested in me, I now pronounce you man and wife. You may salute your bride."

John Ridden turned to Dianne Johnson and said, "Hello Mrs. John Ridden. I will love you always."

The Pastor said, "I now present to you all Mr. and Mrs. John Ridden."

He kissed Dianne with a passion that she never felt before. She knew that John was God sent. Everyone started clapping because they were still kissing. Finally, everyone came and hugged them. There were a lot of wet eyes. The love that John and Dianne had was so surreal. They were so happy that they were now man and wife.

Their wedding was at 6:00 p.m. They ate and danced and had a blessed time. The reception was over at 9:00 p.m. Sheriff John Ridden and Dianne Johnson Ridden thanked everyone for coming. Afterwards Sheriff Ridden and Dianne left the family and went to their new home. The Triplets had helped Dianne furnish their new home. When they got there, he unlocked the door and looked at Dianne and said, "Welcome home Mrs. Ridden."

He picked Dianne up and carried her over the threshold. After they were inside, he kissed her for a long time. The Triplets had made sure that they had groceries in the home, so they wouldn't have to go out in a few days, unless they wanted too. John and Dianne are now married and in their own home. They are so excited and don't know what to do. The night is still young and they are wondering what to do.

Sheriff Ridden asked, "Dianne, I am so overjoyed that you are my wife. Now that I have you, I am scared."

Dianne said, "Scared of what?"

Sheriff Ridden said, "I love you so much and I don't want to be a disappointment to you."

Dianne walked up to him. She said, "John, I love you and I love you for you. You don't need to do or say anything special. I always have loved you."

Sheriff Ridden took her in arms and just held her. He said, "That's why I love you. You are always concerned more about others than yourself. I love you so much that it hurts."

Dianne said, "Come and sit down. We are on a

new highway, but the important thing is, we are going in the same direction. We just got married and we are a little nervous. We have never been together, and it's been years since either of us, have been with anyone sexually. We have plenty of time to get to know each other and it's natural for us to be on edge. Everything is going to be alright."

Sheriff Ridden said, "I feel like this because I am in love with you. For years, I thought that I was never going to be with you. I am so happy until I don't know what to do."

Dianne asked, "Are you hungry? Would you like a glass of water or juice?"

Sheriff Ridden said, "I think I'll take a couple of Tylenol so I can relax a little. I am here with you and still can't believe that we are married."

Dianne said, "We are married. Let's sit here and cuddle for a while."

She turned on the television. She could feel his

body trembling next to her. She turned to him.

Dianne said, "Honey, relax. We are together now. I can feel your body trembling. You are making me nervous."

Sheriff Ridden said, "I am sorry."

Dianne said, "John, we have never been alone like this. We are two adults who have been in love with each other for years. Now it's kind of hard to believe that we are finally together. We don't have to rush. We can go as slow as you want too."

Sheriff Ridden said, "I feel like an idiot. On my wedding night, I am afraid to be with my wife. I never thought anything like this would happen."

Dianne said, "I am going to take a shower and put on something comfortable and take this make-up off my face. You are going to be alright."

Dianne went to the bathroom and took a shower and put on a nice gown and robe. After she finished taking her make-up off, she went into the family room, where Sheriff Ridden was on the couch.

Dianne said, "John go and take a shower and put on your pajamas. I am going to make us a hot cup of cocoa."

Sheriff Ridden said, "All right. Hot cocoa sounds good."

When Sheriff Ridden came out of the bathroom from taking his shower, Dianne had brought their cocoa on a tray in their bedroom. She picked up a cup and gave it to him. They sat on the side of the bed drinking cocoa. Finally, they finished the cocoa. Dianne took their cups and put them on the tray on the dresser.

Then she walked over and stood in front of Sheriff Ridden. She took off her robe and laid it on the foot of the bed. Then she put her arms around Sheriff Ridden neck and kissed him like she had never kissed him before. Naturally he responded without even thinking. Now, he was with the woman that he had always loved. She is his wife and together they were lost in a mood of passion, a feeling that he had never felt before. He was ecstatically happy and found himself crying.

She whispered in his ear, "It's alright my love. We will be together forever."

The next morning Sheriff Ridden was awake before Dianne. He had gotten up, showered and fixed her breakfast in bed. When she woke up, he had just sat the tray on the night stand. She jumped out of bed and ran into the bathroom. She took a quick shower and brushed her teeth. She just put on her robe and nothing under it.

Dianne said, "Good morning darling."

Sheriff Ridden said, "Good morning Mrs. Ridden. I am so sorry about last night."

Dianne said, "There is no need to be but if you are, you can show me how much."

Sheriff Ridden smiled and climbed back in bed,

with her and that's where they spent the next three days in the paradise of their love. After Sheriff Ridden and Dianne had been married for four months, she discovered that she was pregnant. She was so happy because she knew that Sheriff Ridden had wanted children.

When he came home from work that evening, she had a nice meal cooked.

After they finished eating, Dianne said, "I want to talk to you about something."

Sheriff Ridden said, "What is wrong? Are you alright?"

Dianne said, "Yes I am alright. I just want to know how happy are you going to be when I start gaining weight."

Sheriff Ridden said, "Honey I will love you no matter how big you get."

Dianne said, "Even if I get nine months big?"

Sheriff Ridden dropped a glass of juice he was

holding. He wasn't quite sure of what she meant. He got nervous. "What does she mean?

Sheriff Ridden asked, "Wh-at, what do you mean?"

Dianne said, "We are pregnant!"

Sheriff Ridden asked, "Are you kidding me?"

Dianne said, "No way, would I kid you about this. We are six weeks."

Sheriff Ridden hugged Dianne so tight that she had to say, "Honey, I can't breathe."

Sheriff Ridden said, "Oh my god! Thank you, Jesus! Thank you, honey."

Then he fell on the floor crying. He was balding. He could not believe it. Dianne sat on the floor by him and he sat up and was hugging her and still crying.

Dianne said, "It's going to be alright. You are a real Dad, and you will be good with our baby." Then she started crying. She knew how much, this meant to him. They were on the floor for quite a while.

Sheriff Ridden said, "I love you so much and thank you."

Dianne said, "I didn't do it by myself."

They started laughing.

Sheriff Ridden asked, "When will you see the Doctor again?"

Dianne said, "In three weeks."

Sheriff Ridden said, "I want to go with you to all of your appointments."

Dianne said, "When I go again, they will do the ultrasound."

Sheriff Ridden said, "I can't believe it! I am going to be a dad."

When Dianne told the Triplets they could not believe it. They were overjoyed. When Sheriff Ridden told Deputies Carson and Ryan that he was going to be a dad, they were very happy for him. But when he told them that he would be retiring soon, they didn't like that. It had been just the three of them in the office for almost five years.

Dianne didn't plan to tell her family or Sheriff Riddens' family until she saw the Doctor again, to make sure everything was alright. She is almost forty-four years old.

On her next visit, her Doctor ordered an ultrasound.

Dianne's Doctor asked, "Do you all want to know the sex of the baby?"

Sheriff Ridden looked at Dianne as she was looking at him.

The Doctor said, "You don't have to decide right now."

When the Nurse did the ultrasound, she summoned the doctor in the room.

The Doctor said, "You are having Identical Twin boys."

Sheriff Ridden almost fainted. He fell in a chair. The nurse went and got ammonia for him to breathe.

Sheriff Ridden asked, "Doctor is the ultra sound accurate?"

The Doctor said, "It is very accurate and your sons look very healthy."

Dianne started crying. She said, "Identical Twin boys!"

She was thinking when she had the Triplets and one of them was stolen.

The Doctor said, "Mrs. Ridden you are very healthy, but don't be lifting anything heavy. There is no reason for you to be concerned about any problems."

Sheriff Ridden said, "Honey, I want you to get plenty of rest every day. I will hire a maid to do, the house cleaning."

Dianne said, "Mr. Ridden, I am pregnant, not an invalid. I will not be doing anything strenuous or lifting anything heavy."

They thanked the Doctor. Her next visit will be in three weeks.

Dianne said, "Now you can tell your family that you are a dad, and I will tell my family that we are having Identical Twin boys."

Sheriff Ridden said, "I can't believe it! I finally got the woman that I love and now I am going to be a dad."

Dianne said, "You will be a great dad."

Sheriff Ridden said, "There is something that I need to tell you."

Dianne asked, "What is it?"

Sheriff Ridden said, "I am going to retire from being a Sheriff."

Dianne asked, "What brought this on? Are you alright John?"

Sheriff Ridden said, "I am fine. Now that I am going to be a dad, I don't want a job where every time I leave home, I will be worried if I will make it back home."

Dianne asked, "Are you sure that's what you want to do? You know something could happen to you at home."

Sheriff Ridden said, "I can't explain what it means to me to be a dad. It's something that I have always wanted."

Dianne said, "John, God has brought us together after all, of these years. I never even thought about getting pregnant when we got married. I have never used birth control. It never crossed my mind that I might get pregnant, but it didn't matter, because they are our babies and God gave them to us. I believe in my heart that he will let you see them grow up."

Sheriff Ridden said, "You are right, but I feel that I need to do this. I will at least take some time off when our babies arrive."

Dianne said, "Do me a favor, let us pray and ask God what you should do."

Sheriff Ridden said, "Alright we will pray and I will wait for an answer."

As time passed and Dianne went into labor and gave birth to two handsome Identical Twin boys. They were named Bryan and Ryan Ridden. They were born July 30, 2007. Sheriff Ridden was telling everyone that he was a Dad. The Triplets were just as happy as Sheriff Ridden. One day they were all together and the Triplets told Sheriff Ridden, that they have to stop calling him Sheriff and call him dad. His eyes watered.

Dianne said, "Watch out for the tears. He loves you guys so much and now that he has two sons, he's overjoyed."

As the boys began to crawl around and call Sheriff Ridden, Da-da, he was in heaven. This was a turning point in his life that he never expected. Since he didn't have Dianne, he just assumed that he would grow old by himself. But God! It shows if you are obedient and trust God, you will always be surprised at the things He does in your life.

Sheriff Ridden, Dianne, the Triplets and the Twin boys are happy. Now that the Triplets have found the Organization of Multi Births, they have met a nice set of male Triplets. Who knows, maybe soon they will be getting married. Jesus is the greatest joy in life and family is next.

DORIS' PUBLISHED WORKS

I'll WAIT **(Romance)**

Who Did It? **(Mystery)**

Love Has No Color **(Romance)**

Thoughts of Mind **(Poetry)**

A Girl Named Sarah **(Little Girl's Faith)**

How to Survive on a Little **(How to)**

The Pirates Who Found Jesus **(Inspirational)**

Joe's Most Dangerous Mission **(Fantasy)**

Thoughts Feelings Visions Memories **(Poetry)**

Future Works

Get to Know Your Body **(Health)**

Invisible Molly **(Fantasy)**

BIO OF DORIS M. JONES

Doris was born and raised in Dallas, Texas. She is second of seven children. As a child she was very bashful. She is a mother, grand-mother and great-grandmother.

She lives in Sothern California. Doris has been writing since she was a child (Poetry), and short stories in high school.

She was selected Who's Who in Poetry for 2004-2005. She has many written reviews from people who have read most of her books. She has many Merits of Honor, Editor's Choice, Awards, etc.

Doris has about seventy poems published in different Poetry Anthologies in the Public Libraries under Doris M. Jones-Landrine (her previous married name). Two of her poems were published in The Fresno Bee when she lived in Fresno, CA.

DORIS' ACCOMPLISHMENTS

CAREGIVER

PUBLISHED POET

PUBLISHED AUTHOR (IN SIX GENRES)

PROPERTY MANAGER (LICENSED FOR CALIF.)

MEDICAL ASSISTANT, RECEPTIONIST AND SCHEDULER

(THESE ARE GOALS THAT I SET FOR MY LIFE THAT GOD
ALLOWED TO COME TO FRUITION.)